THE BLACKSMITH

Order of the Broken Blade

CECELIA MECCA

Altiora Press

Dear Readers,

*Thank you for pledging your troth to me.
I will be forever grateful.*

Cecelia

JOIN OUR SECRET ORDER

We may not be knights intent on toppling a monarchy, but the Blood and Brawners are certainly one fun group of romance readers who enjoy being teased (actually, that drives them crazy but I do it anyway) and chatting all things romance and hunky heroes.

Facebook.com/Groups/BloodandBrawn

The Order of the Broken Blade - OBB

Conrad - Earl of Licheford

Lance - blacksmith, knighted (begin this) by Conrad

Terric (not english, a Baron's son, clan chief of clan kennaugh) of Bradon Moor / Lord Dromsley in England

Guy (mercenary, knight, greatest sword in England Lavall(is?) of Cradney Wrens

1

Northumbria, England, 1214

"This is treason."

Lance said it first and wasn't surprised when no one responded. They all knew it, and speaking the word aloud again would serve no purpose.

"Think carefully before you respond." Conrad moved to the flap of the tent, peered outside, and apparently satisfied, sat back down.

So *this* was why his friend had set up so far away from the rest of the tents. Conrad had known that his proposal would turn the four of them into traitors.

"I'll do it," he said.

The earl would only have proposed such a drastic action after careful consideration, and he trusted his friend implicitly.

All three of the men watched him, none more carefully than Conrad. But he had said his piece. He wouldn't change his mind.

"We will need support." Terric had more reason to march against the king than any of them, but he was also the most cautious. He would have the most questions, but Lance was confident he would do it. They all would.

"If the Northern lords don't join together now," Conrad said, "then they are lost."

"We'll be lost too, lest you forget." Guy crossed his arms and sat back in the chair that had been carted here on a wagon filled with the luxuries afforded them by Conrad's station.

Their friend cared little for such comforts, which was why it had surprised Lance when he'd insisted on attending the Tournament of the North in such a stately fashion, something his father would have done were he still alive. Conrad was reminding those who might join their cause that the Earl of Licheford was one of the most powerful Northern border lords.

"I am no great lord," Guy continued, "but I'm as affected by John's policies as any."

"And taxes," Conrad added. "His policies and taxes. Both will be our demise if we allow it."

Guy shrugged as if their friend had asked if he wished for a meal rather than suggested they join forces against their king. "I'd not turn away an adventure such as this."

"An adventure?" Terric shook his head. "You're mad to call it one." Then, turning back to Conrad, "You have a plan?"

"The beginnings of one, aye. The most crucial part being your support."

By "your" he meant the three of them. With just one more assent, the course of each of their lives would change forever.

Terric stood and extended his arm, fist clenched. His friend had extended his arm for such a vow only once before.

Conrad clasped his wrist.

Guy was next.

Lance, last.

"Today we pledge more than a vow of silence. We form an order this day." Conrad looked directly at Terric. "The Order of the Broken Blade."

A perfect name. A symbol of the abuse of power that can accompany a man who believes his rule divine. Nothing but silence followed his proclamation.

It was more than a name. It was a *promise*. Like the first one they made to one another many, many years ago. No one else would understand the significance, yet each of them did—and each took it to heart.

"For England," Terric said. Ironic for him to be the one to say so, as he was the only one among them not English.

Lance hated to dissent but thought it important to mention a fact Conrad seemed to have overlooked.

"An order? Of knights?"

Unclasping hands, they waited for him to finish.

"Surely you see the problem? Aye, you're an earl, and Terric's a baron's son." He nodded to Guy. "Even the mercenary is a knight."

"And my title is well earned," Guy winked, "unlike these two."

Lance couldn't help but smile at that. Guy had made the remark many times over the years. That it failed to rile Conrad now was a mark of the seriousness of their discussion.

"Take out your sword," Conrad ordered, his gaze on Lance.

There were few men Lance took orders from these days, but this man was one of them. So he complied.

He'd intended to remind Conrad he was but a blacksmith, but there was no use telling his friends what they already knew. And though Lance had no use for a fancy title or any of its trappings, the solemnity of the moment was not lost on him. No, it was clear to them all. One look at Terric's and Guy's expressions told him as much.

Ignoring the others, he dropped to one knee, laying his sword across it as Conrad pulled out his own sword. Tapping him on each shoulder, he uttered the words Lance had never thought to hear in his lifetime. When he was finished, Conrad bade him rise.

"Stand up as a knight, in the name of God."

He did, unsure what to say.

"Do you have any further opposition to our order?" Conrad asked.

"No."

"Good. We've much to discuss."

Of that, Lance had no doubt. Rebelling against a king required planning, after all.

"Including your new title." Guy bowed to him. "Sir Lance."

"I quite like it." Terric bowed as well.

"A Scots clan chief bowing to an English blacksmith." Guy looked at Conrad, raising his eyebrows dramatically. "I'll admit 'tis a sight I'll not soon forget."

"When you finish jesting . . ."

"Does he ever?" Lance asked Conrad sincerely.

"We've the small matter of King John to discuss."

Small matter indeed. If even a hint of what they'd just done were whispered to the wrong person, their heads would be forfeit for it.

Knight or blacksmith, earl or mercenary . . . none of their titles, or lack thereof, would matter if they were exposed as traitors to the crown.

THE KING'S MEN MARCHED THROUGH THE courtyard as if it were their own. Idalia's father stood next to her on the doorstep of the great keep's entrance. She peeked up at him, wondering when the hair of his beard had become more gray than black.

"Welcome," he boomed as the first of the newcomers reached them. A captain, perhaps? Idalia tried not to smile at the looks they were receiving. Not outright hostility, but certainly the people of Stanton could give the representatives of the king a warmer welcome.

She was secretly glad they did not.

"My lord." The tall, thin captain bowed to her father, the Earl of Stanton. "We travel to Norham Castle and request shelter for the evening."

Interesting. Why were the king's men on their way to Norham and so far north?

Idalia could hear her father's silent answer to her silent question. *Do not concern yourself with the affairs of men.* She also knew what he would say next.

"My daughter will see to your comfort." He looked at her as if expecting a retort. It was market day, her favorite, and Father knew it well.

But he knew his daughter too.

"Of course." She smiled as the captain and his two companions joined her. They were dressed identically, in armor topped with bright red tunics bearing the crest of their king. They'd require assistance in removing that armor. Marina, her mother's maid, would normally assist her in making the arrangements, but Marina was nowhere to be seen.

More likely than not, she was sitting at Idalia's mother's bedside, something the maid often chided her for doing.

I have been her maid for as many years as you are alive, she would say. Which was not fully correct—Idalia had only been alive for two and twenty years, and Marina had been her mother's most trusted servant for four years longer. Sometimes it felt as if Idalia had two mothers.

"Follow me," she instructed the men, catching her father's small smile. Seeing one of his rare smiles almost made missing market day worthwhile.

Taking them past the great stairs on either side of the entranceway to the keep, Idalia nearly missed the flash of royal blue.

Her younger sister. She wished to call out to Tilly, but it was unlikely she'd get a response. Tilly disliked helping with the duties about Stanton. Sure enough, the flash of blue was there and then gone.

By the time she showed the men to their chambers and sent up a squire to assist them with their armor, Dawson, the seneschal, had already spoken to Cook about dinner and arranged baths for the three men.

His help had eased the burden of the unexpected guests, but Idalia had one more thing to do before she could check on her mother. The captain had made a special request of her—or rather, of the smith. She left the great keep and walked through the courtyard down to the castle forge. Stepping around puddles that had formed on the gravel path after that morning's rain, she arrived, the door, as always, already open.

"Daryon," she said, stepping into the darkened room. "Is there enough light to repair a shoe?"

The apprentice looked up, hammer in hand. His brother had already begun tidying up. It was a habit Roland had instilled in his apprentices. Idalia pushed the thought away. When she thought of how the blacksmith had suffered before he'd succumbed to an illness all had known would claim him someday, a familiar pang in her chest reminded her of the master smith's absence.

"Aye, my lady." He looked at her hand.

"I don't have it with me but will send it straightaway. 'Tis for the king's captain," she added.

"Shall I fetch it from the stables?" the lad's twin brother, Miles, asked. At only ten and two, the boys were carrying a responsibility that should never have been asked of them. Two apprentices smithing for a castle the size of Stanton . . . she shook her head. The situation could have been avoided had her father taken Roland's illness more seriously. They should have started looking for a new master smith long ago.

"Aye, thank you. The new master should be arriving any day now." A replacement smith had finally been found at this year's Tournament of the North, a yearly event where English knights and Scottish warriors prepared for the very real battles they would later fight.

She wanted the boys to know their hard work had not gone unnoticed. "My father is grateful for your service in the interim."

As expected, both boys beamed at the praise. And it was true. Although her father rarely seemed to notice her own service to Stanton, he did recognize the boys were much too young for their current position. They were only in their third year of seven in training.

Daryon watched his brother leave. Unlike most others in the keep, Idalia could easily tell the two boys apart, and it was that look that made it so easy. Daryon was by far the more serious of the two.

The boy's thoughtful eyes darted from the doorway to her. "'Tis market day."

And Idalia never missed one if she had the choice.

"Aye, but we must see to our royal visitors," she said.

Three years earlier, her father had received a charter for Stanton to be designated a market town, courtesy of the well-maintained old Roman roads that led both north and south as well as east and west. Many castles did not enjoy such a right, especially in the "wilds" of Northern England, and Idalia was grateful for their good fortune. She visited the market as one of her duties for Stanton—her mother was much too ill to do so. Secretly, she also hoped she would one day find the herb or tonic that might help her mother. The market attracted all sorts, after all. To make such inquiries directly was impossible, however, as her father had forbidden her from speaking of her mother's worsening condition to anyone.

"Had I known, I would have gone yesterday," she said. The market day was actually poorly named—it had grown in popularity enough to stretch to two days. "And if the new master does not have the drift you need, I promise to secure your tool on the next market day."

"Thank you, my lady."

She could tell Daryon was anxious to get back to work, so she left him to it, intent on visiting with her mother before supper.

And that was when she saw him, the most handsome man she'd ever seen, striding downhill toward the forge.

Toward her.

2

L ance didn't need to be told where the forge was located. He could sense it. Smell it.

He was a blacksmith's son. An apprentice. A journeyman. And a master smith. He'd spent his life sweltering next to a furnace, never imagining that very profession could be the key to saving his country.

According to the other members of the order, anyway. Others would disagree, including the very man they aimed to bring to heel. The one who claimed a divine right to rule—King John Lackland.

Leaving the wagon he'd carted near the stables with his horse, Lance had gone off in search of the seneschal but spied the forge's smoke first. By its position, close to the nearby stream, he assumed it had been built away from the other buildings to allow better access to the fresh water needed to quench the metal.

Though he had a secret purpose for accepting this position as Stanton Castle's next master blacksmith, the fact that Stanton's smithy was kept away from the keep came as a relief nonetheless. When the building occupied a prominent a position in a castle courtyard, there tended to be more interruptions to his work.

"Yer the new smith?"

Lance turned to see an older man regarding him with the same open suspicion as everyone else he'd encountered so far, from the villagers to the guards to the stable master.

Either the people of Stanton had an innate mistrust of strangers or the former smith had been much loved. Or both.

"Aye," he said. "Lance Wayland. Pleased to make your acquaintance."

The castle servant mumbled, "Well met," as he walked away.

Lance stared after him for a moment, the man's red cheeks reminding him of his father. He shook off the association, forcing himself to unclench his fists, and turned back toward his destination. He would find the seneschal later. Since the forge was on the way to the keep, he could not resist a quick visit.

For a castle this size, he'd have thought more people would be milling around the courtyard. He started down the incline, and stopped short at the unexpected sight of a lady standing just outside the forge, her long, golden brown hair sweeping down her back and over her shoulders. A noblewoman to be sure. As surprising as her presence was her smile. Unlike the others he'd met here so far, her expression was purely welcoming. She looked as the first flower of spring might—unexpected, but more beautiful for it, especially after a long winter without color.

He continued downward, aware of her eyes watching his every move.

"Good day," she said, her voice soft and lilting as if she sang rather than spoke the words.

Everything about her face was delicate . . . her nose, her lips, her brows. But as the distance between them closed, he noticed one thing that stood out from the rest.

Her eyes.

Kind. Compassionate.

A man such as he could lose himself in their depths.

"You are the new smith?" she asked.

Though he lacked the smithy's apron, he'd been told many times that he had a blacksmith's build.

Like my father.

He liked to think the only similarity they shared was skin-deep.

"Aye, my lady . . ."

She smiled again as she filled in the gap he'd left. "Idalia. I am the earl's daughter."

"Lady Idalia, then." Her name suited her. A lovely name for a lovely woman. "I am called Lancelin Wayland of Marwood."

Of course, it had been some time since he'd been back to Marwood. There was nothing left for him there now.

"Master Lancelin, then."

"Lance, to my friends."

"A worthy name. Shall I show you to the forge?"

Her manners befitted her station, and as Lance followed the lady down toward the large stone building, certainly larger than any he'd worked in before, he couldn't help watching her walk. Surefooted despite the wet ground beneath them, she held her head high.

As a noblewoman does.

Which should remind you not to stare at her backside.

"'Tis a wonder you were available to come to Stanton Castle. We feared, after Roland passed, it would be some time before a master smith could be found."

Stanton's need for a smith had been the order's good fortune.

"My father said you approached him at the Tournament of the North?"

He caught up with her then, and they slowed as they reached the forge.

"Indeed, my lady."

"Was Lord Bohun very disappointed you left?"

His former master and now ally was actually quite pleased as Lance had told him of his purpose at Stanton, but that fact was one of many Lady Idalia could not know about.

"Aye, my lady, but the opportunity to serve as a castle smith was one I could not ignore." At least part of his statement was true. "I hope to forge more swords and armor than keys and nails here."

She peered inside the shop. "You've two fine young apprentices who are quite adept, so you should definitely find yourself supplementing the armorer here."

That surprised him. "Stanton has its own armorer, then?"

"Nay." She shook her head. "We are supplied by Kenshire's. The old smith, Roland, had little experience forging weapons. I am surprised you are experienced with both."

"My . . ." He nearly said father. "My original master apprenticed in an armory but moved to Marwood as a journeyman."

"And so we are lucky to have you here at Stanton."

When she moved toward him, he could smell a hint of citrus. "I would forewarn you, though. Roland was much loved by the people here. Some may find it . . . difficult to see him replaced. Even by such a fine man as yourself."

Fine? Lance had been described many ways before. Reticent. Unforgiving. But never "fine." He liked the word, especially from her lips.

"I will strive to please my lady and the people of Stanton."

He'd meant nothing by it, but as soon as the words left his mouth, Lance held his breath. He could not afford any missteps here, even a subtle flirtation such as that.

Fortunately, Lady Idalia did not seem to question his choice of words. Pleasing her would be equally enjoyable and disastrous.

For them both.

IDALIA MADE HER WAY BACK TO THE KEEP BUT stopped just before entering. Preparations for the meal would be nearly complete, and she needed a moment to herself.

Waiting until Father Sica moved out of her path, the priest's expression grim as usual, she hurried to the abandoned Small Tower and used one of only two keys that opened the door. Pulling it closed behind her, Idalia hurried up the tightly wound, circular stairs to the top.

This tower was originally meant to be one of four lookouts located at each of the four corners of the inner curtain wall. But before the construction could be completed, her great-grandfather was given a new commission from the king, one that came with a large enough sum to allow him to build a second, and much taller, wall around the first. The towers had instead been placed around the new outer wall, leaving Small Tower an unused anomaly.

Idalia had been coming here since she was a child. All knew of her very poor hiding spot, but only Dawson had another key. And it had been some time since he'd climbed these steep steps. The pain in his knees prevented him from doing so. Once, her mother had wondered aloud if a new, younger seneschal might replace him. Her father had not taken kindly to the suggestion and none had mentioned it since.

But she'd not come here to dwell on her mother's illness. Reaching the top of the tower, Idalia leaned against the cold stone wall and closed her eyes, imagining him.

She'd spoken to Lance but once. Still, she could envision his face clearly.

Although he didn't have a beard, he'd not shaven for some days, the whiskers on his face as black as the tousled waves that came down to the tips of his ears and covered his entire forehead.

Built like a knight, nay, a blacksmith, he was difficult to miss and she'd certainly not done so. She'd stopped walking the moment she'd caught sight of him.

He'd done the same.

He'd looked at her as if she were beautiful, but she knew the truth, just like everyone around Stanton did. She was naught but a plainer version of her very beautiful older sister. As her younger sister, too young to know any better, had once said, she was "pretty enough."

Well, he was much more than ordinary.

I really should get back to the keep.

Just one more moment, she negotiated with herself.

Idalia opened her eyes, staring at the wall in front of her. Others might have a moment to spare for daydreams, but she did not. Standing up straight, she sighed and began the careful walk back down the stairs.

Would Tilly be back from market day? No doubt that was where she'd run off to earlier, pretending not to have seen her. At ten and four, her sister could be trusted with some tasks, but she could never be completely relied upon. Indeed, she was still a child in many ways, and if Idalia could help it, she'd remain so for as long as possible.

Though she would have liked a sachet of citrus blossom and a few other supplies.

As she locked the tower door, two hands covered her eyes from behind. Had her thoughts summoned her sister?

"Do not look," Tilly said, taking her hands away. "Close your eyes."

"I assumed that was what you meant me to do when you told me not to look."

"Smell."

The directive wasn't needed. She'd already caught the scent. Smiling, she took the sachet from under her nose and turned around.

"Thank you, Till."

She looked down at the almoner pouch wondering what else her sister had picked up from the market.

"What did you . . ." She stopped as Tilly pulled two bulbs of garlic from her pouch. How many items did she have in there? "'Tis said if you peel it and place it under the pillow, it may help to relieve a headache."

Idalia crossed her arms and waited.

"I knew you would be angry. But Idalia, she is in so much pain."

"And if the merchant asks questions?"

"He will not." She tucked the garlic back inside. "I've not seen him before. Likely never will again." Tilly rolled her eyes. "I didn't say, 'Can you please help with a remedy for my mother.'"

"Shhh," she scolded. Though the courtyard was not as busy as normal with supper approaching, there were still plenty of servants and men-at-arms moving around them. "Father will not be pleased."

Even if Idalia did not fully agree with her father's

insistence on keeping the extent of their mother's illness secret, she understood his concern. And though she herself sought potential cures, Tilly had not quite mastered the art of subtlety. All would know her purpose for the garlic bulbs before long.

Father Sica had hinted, as her mother's pain increased, that her condition was a spiritual matter that could be treated by no physician—a test from Satan. Idalia knew her father feared the priest would bring his talk of Satan's influence to the village. He worried such aspersions would ruin not just his wife's reputation, but the prospects of his two marriageable daughters. He was an earl, a powerful Northumbrian lord who once served as judicar to the king, and yet priests had a power all their own.

If she or her sisters criticized the priest, however, her father would say only, "He is a man of God."

Idalia sighed. Though her father relied on her, he refused to listen to her counsel on most subjects, their mother chief among them.

"He will not know," her conspiratorial sister replied.

They'd just entered the great keep, and as expected, her absence had been missed.

"Lady Idalia . . . if you'll pardon us, Lady Tilly," said the laundress. "The new girl," she said, wringing her hands.

"Aye? What of her?"

Tilly used the interruption to wander away, as was her custom.

"She broke a paddle. After comin' back from market without the lye soap I asked her for."

"Have you spoken to Dawson?"

Though she asked, Idalia already knew the answer. Although the seneschal was officially in charge of the household staff, everyone came to her first. It had been that way for some time, even when Roysa, her older sister, was still in residence. Roysa had since wed a powerful border baron.

"Nay, my lady. Shall I do so?" the older woman asked, blinking. It was an open secret that the laundress was slightly terrified of him.

"I will speak to the girl. But," Idalia warned, "you will need to practice patience as well. She is still young."

The laundress was already nodding, grateful. "Aye, my lady."

And so it went until Idalia resigned herself to visiting her mother after the meal rather than before it.

It was only when the second course was served she thought again of the new smith.

Idalia knew in some households he would not be invited to eat here in the hall. But at Stanton Castle, all were welcome, courtesy of her mother. She'd insisted, for as long as Idalia could remember, that anyone who contributed to the well-being of their home had a place at every meal.

She was about to send an invitation to him when the very man she was thinking about strode into the hall.

And looked directly at her.

3

L ance had never met a more suspicious lot.

He sat at the back corner of the hall, pleased to learn he had a place there but less so about the dour looks he received. Though none would accuse him of being overly gregarious, Lance could usually befriend the locals quite easily.

Not so the people of Stanton.

Forcing himself to ignore the dais, he listened to the workers who sat around him.

"They came today, but no one knows their purpose here," said one man deep in his cups.

"They?" he asked.

All turned to stare at him.

"Lance," he said to those he had not yet met, answering the unasked question. "Wayland. The new smith."

Grunts and one half-mumbled "Aye" was what he'd expected and what he received.

Lady Idalia had warned him, but the old blacksmith must have been even more beloved than she'd thought. Lance understood such loyalty. This wasn't the first time he'd replaced an old master. But this time, there was much more at stake.

"He talks of the king's men."

This from the redhead at the end of their trestle table.

"I'm Robert, the butler," he added.

So this was the man in charge of Stanton's stores of ale. An important position, and one who would make him a good ally.

The meaning of the butler's words penetrated as he lifted his own mug of ale to his lips. "Did you say the king's men?" he asked, lowering it.

His gaze shot to the area just below the dais. Shifting to see between the other hundred or so retainers that dined between them, Lance spotted the distinct red and yellow of the men's surcoats.

Without reacting, he turned back to his meal.

But not before getting a glimpse of her.

She sat next to her father, as regal as a queen. Not that he'd ever *seen* a queen before, but he had been around plenty of noblewomen, and Lady Idalia was certainly that.

Which only served as a reminder that he needed to stay well away from her.

"Is it common for the king's men to visit here?" He addressed the question to the butler since none of the others seemed inclined to include him in the conversation.

In answer, Robert shrugged.

He wouldn't make further inquiries yet, but the presence of these men did not bode well for his mission here. If the earl received the king's representatives regularly, it might be an unwelcome clue to his political leanings.

If Lance and his friends were to rebel against the most powerful man in the country, one whose ruthless extortion of his barons had prompted them to form the order, they would need the Earl of Stanton's support. Without it, they had little chance of bringing King John to heel.

That Stanton had needed a new blacksmith just when they needed powerful allies had been either a lucky happenstance or a sign. While he was glad for it, Lance did not necessarily agree with Conrad, who'd suggested it was divine fate. "The fates clear a path to the one man who will convince all others," he'd said after sharing the entirety of his plan to him in that tent. That plan had led him here.

"Go back to London," the man sitting next to him muttered, presumably to the king's men.

None responded, but it was the opening Lance needed.

"Nord."

It was a risk. A Nord battle cry. More than a word.

When he was answered with grunts and nods, Lance breathed more easily. These were Northerners like him, but that did not mean their lord was on his side.

Unlike some of the others who had declared publicly against John after his most recent defeat in France, Stanton had remained silent on the matter. According to Conrad, whose father and Stanton had disliked each other so intensely Conrad could not risk approaching the man himself, the earl's father had served the king well. The son had done the same, back when Henry was still king. He'd even served as his judicar.

But that had been before John. Before the taxes that increased so often, for a failed war with France, his men could no longer pay them. Before the kidnappings, John's answer to his barons' inability to pay constantly increasing taxes. Just before the tournament yet another baron's daughter had been taken by the king's men after her father refused to pay twenty thousand marks for permission to secure her marriage. Before the aggression on his own people— the barons and earls in the north who had begun to take a stand.

Lance remained silent for the remainder of the meal. It had been an eventful first day, and he knew when to retreat.

He also knew better than to look up at the dais again. But although he was a disciplined man, and a smart one, the instinct was too strong to be denied.

❧

THE SUMMER SUN SHONE BRIGHT, A WELCOME relief from the rain of the past three days. It was nearing time for dinner, but their royal guests had just departed, leaving Idalia a few moments of respite. She'd already attended mass and visited with her mother, who now lay on two heads of garlic under her pillow courtesy of Tilly. After speaking to cook about provisions for the day and seeking out the tutor to discuss her sister, who'd missed another lesson that morn, she'd decided a visit to the forge was necessary.

It is my duty to see to the smith as I would any worker in the castle. It has naught to do with how he looked at me last eve.

She knew that was not altogether true, but it wasn't a fabrication either. The marshal had asked for the help of one or both of the boys at the smithy. Two of the stable boys had fallen ill, both on the same day.

As she approached the forge, smoke billowed out of the stone building. She thought of Roland, who had served Stanton Castle since before she was born. The people were not alone in their grief over losing him.

"The impurities will crack off as you twist it."

The low voice reached her ears as she came to a stop in the open doorway. Miles and Daryon stood watching, transfixed, as the new smith leaned over the anvil, his back to her. She could see the awe on the boys' faces and wondered what Lance was about.

Idalia took a step inside, somewhat accustomed to the heat in the tool-lined space. Roland's work had always fascinated her, and she'd spent more time down here than her father would have liked.

"Master Roland never twisted a nail before," Miles said to the smith.

She took another step toward them, and froze.

Lance's arms were bare. Covered in soot but very, very bare. As he held up his handiwork, muscled biceps and thick forearms moving in unison, she could not help but admire his form. And though she quickly looked away, toward the bright orange metal clasped between the tongs he held, she could tell by his expression she'd been caught.

He didn't smile, exactly, but the corners of his mouth lifted ever so slightly.

"He could twist a metal rod," Daryon clarified, "but that nail is so small."

"It's called a rope twist," Lance said, still looking at her.

Idalia swallowed. She'd never minded the heat in the forge before, but suddenly it engulfed her. As did his stare. She couldn't look away.

He finally broke the stare, turning to his young apprentices.

Her shoulders fell. Idalia could breathe again.

Of sorts.

"This is a very special nail," Lance said. "I'll be showing you a new technique each day."

He dropped the nail to the side and handed Miles his pliers.

"Can you spare the boys until midday?" Idalia asked, remembering the marshal's plea. "Our marshal finds himself without two stable boys and could use assistance grooming this morn."

Lance nodded to the boys. "Go."

They obeyed immediately, scurrying past her and out the door.

"I fear your gown will be worse for visiting here," he said.

Indeed, her pale yellow frock would collect soot more easily than most, earning her a lecture from the laundress, but it would not be her first talking-to.

"I'm no stranger to the forge," she said, watching him wipe his hands on a cloth that was more black than cream. A leather apron fit snugly around his chest, but it was his arms that captured her attention.

Not that Idalia had never seen a man's bare arms before. She had, especially here in this forge. But this was the first time she'd ever wished to run her hands over them before.

"'Tis unusual for a lady, is it not?"

She looked up quickly.

"Aye. But I was quite close with Roland."

Lance leaned against a table where tools lay scattered. They were everywhere. Hanging on the walls, covering each surface. But it was precisely that disorder that had always appealed to her, a refreshing change from her so very structured life.

"You said he was beloved here."

"His father served as blacksmith before him."

Had she imagined the dark look that passed over his features? The new smith seemed to smile little, but her remark had displeased him somehow. Was it because he'd been met with a cool reception?

"I can help you," she blurted out.

He stared at her, his expression indiscernible.

"Ingrain yourself here in Stanton," she clarified. "We celebrate with the Gule of August feast in three days' time. The keep will be filled as the farmers come with their offerings, and all are welcome to join the feast. 'Tis a custom for the craftsmen to offer my

23

father a token of their finest work. Show him, every-one, what you can do."

"In three days?"

"Admittedly it is not much time, and there are those who do not participate." She shrugged her shoulders. "'Tis not required of you to do so."

"But you believe I should?"

"Aye."

"Why would you help me?"

She hadn't expected the question. Why indeed?

"'Tis what I do," she said simply. A true enough statement.

He shifted his position, his arms reaching down to grab the edge of the table. Which was when she no-ticed the design on his left arm. She'd never seen any-thing quite like it.

"What is it?" she asked, moving closer. The black mark was etched into the skin across his upper arm. But it was only when he twisted it a bit that she could see the design clearly.

"The fleur-de-lis."

An odd marking for an English blacksmith. Be-fore she realized what she was doing, Idalia reached out as if to touch it, pulling back at the last moment.

"Go on," he said.

His eyes were brown. A deep, dark brown that seemed appropriate to his visage. To his intensity too.

"I would not be so bold," she said, her cheeks warming at the realization she'd nearly touched him.

"I believe you would."

Her head snapped up at that.

"Go on," he prompted again, still holding his arm out to her.

Although she knew she should do otherwise—she should leave and never come back—she reached a tentative finger up to trace the delicate design. She'd expected it to be raised but instead it felt like . . .

skin. Hard, warm. And for some reason, she traced the design in its entirety, as if memorizing the details.

"'Tis beautiful."

She pulled her hand away.

"Aye."

Lance was looking directly at her as he said it. That look gripped her, sending the oddest sensation through her entire body, right down to her core.

Desire.

Idalia put some distance between them, stepping back.

"What does it mean?"

He opened his mouth, as if to tell her, when a familiar voice called to her from outside.

"Idalia? There you are. Dawson is asking for you. And Cook needs a word."

Her chest rose and fell as she looked between Lance and her sister.

"This is our new smith, Master Lance. I'm pleased to introduce my sister, Lady Tilly," she said.

"Well met," her sister said, nodding toward the door. Her gaze only briefly lingered on Lance, as if she did not realize he was the most compelling man who'd ever set foot in Stanton. "You're needed at the keep."

Always.

Smiling at the smith, Idalia wondered at his grim expression as she followed her sister out into the sun. Away from the darkness of the blacksmith's shop. Away from the blacksmith himself.

A dangerous man, to be sure, in more ways than one.

4

He'd not seen her since their interaction in the forge three days earlier.

Lance stood in the back of the great hall, waiting for his turn to present the item in his hands to the earl. This would be his first contact with the man their order so desperately needed. Without his support, their mission was sure to falter.

As the other skilled workers presented their handiwork to the earl, Lance kept his eyes on the dais. They sat in a row. The earl, Lady Idalia, her younger sister, and then an empty seat, presumably the one typically occupied by Lady Emmeline.

He'd not learned much about the countess, other than that she was ill, and had been for some time. Some even said she was dying.

As Idalia had predicted, the people of Stanton were not eager to welcome the replacement for their beloved former smith. The situation was complicated by the fact that Conrad had urged him to make haste.

His friend's directive had been clear.

Go to Stanton Castle. Speak to its people, discern the earl's leanings. If it was as they suspected, his name having been whispered among John's dissenters, garner his support for their cause.

"The new smith is presenting to Lord Stanton."

Although he couldn't see who'd spoken, Lance heard the approval behind the remark. The boys had told him how important this feast was to the people of Stanton. According to Miles, the harvest was so poor one year, many had died of starvation. Though he had been just a babe at the time, his mother had told the boys of the horrors that had brought Stanton, and its people, to its knees. The next year, after a harvest that had helped the land and people recover, they'd celebrated the Gule of August for the first time. It had felt like the miracle Stanton needed—and so, a sacred new tradition had started.

Had he not participated in the festivities, Lance would likely have found his position here even more tenuous than it was already.

I can help you. It's what I do.

He could not take his eyes off her, despite knowing he should. It had become clear to him, both in their brief interactions and what he'd heard over the last few days, that she was every bit the lady of the castle. She'd assumed her mother's responsibilities with an elegance and ease everyone admired.

When she'd touched his arm that day, Lance had realized his attraction to her was no simple problem. If her father suspected the new smith woke in the night to visions of his daughter, a very proper noble lady, lying beneath him, more than his position at Stanton would be at stake.

With that thought in mind, he tore his gaze from her to focus on the father.

Lance had first seen the earl at the Tournament of the North many years earlier. The earl no longer participated, but, like many of the older nobles, he saw the tournament as an opportunity to strengthen old alliances and forge new ones.

Lance smiled at the thought. It had certainly done that for him. For the Order.

"A right old bastard," Conrad had called him, though none at Stanton seemed to hold his friend's same opinion. Indeed, he was as beloved as the old smith. But since Conrad was predisposed to dislike the earl, owing to his own father's feud with Lord Stanton, Lance would have to assess the man solely on his own merit.

He was next.

A bright blue banner with a single gold lion in its center covered the wall behind the earl's family. Lance shook off the similarity to John's coat of arms, knowing both symbols had been created long before either man was born.

Even so, the similarity, especially coupled with the fact that the king's men had recently paid a visit to Stanton, was disconcerting.

"Master Lance Wayland, the new smith," the tall, older seneschal announced.

Avoiding Idalia's gaze, Lance instead looked directly into the eyes of the Earl of Stanton. Neither of them smiled. He bowed and awaited instruction.

"Wayland?" Stanton's tone was deep and strong. An earl's voice. "You've much to live up to, then," he said, referring to his name.

"And will do so, my lord."

A bold claim, to match the skill of a mythological smith said to have forged more than seven hundred rings for his king.

But also a fine introduction for the unusual piece he'd brought with him.

"I arrived less than a fortnight ago but am pleased to present this piece to my lord."

He handed the bracelet to the seneschal, still watching the earl—which meant he knew the exact moment the earl realized it was not, in fact, for him.

"A gift for a woman worthy of it."

He could see people on either side of him straining to get a look at the piece. The chatter began almost immediately, as he'd expected it would.

If Lance had learned anything in his years of service to fine lords, it was that a nobleman such as Stanton needed no gifts. Nor was he as worthy to receive them as the woman who'd borne his children.

Or, in this case, the child who had grown into a woman herself.

He let the earl incorrectly assume he'd made the iron bracelet, a delicate piece of twisted metal that very few could achieve, as an offering for the countess.

You play with fire.

Lance would have smiled were he ever inclined to do so. Aye, it had been a bold move—a risky one too. But so was their plan.

"You forged this here?"

The earl turned the bracelet around in his hands.

"I did, my lord."

When he looked up, it was with the new respect Lance needed to earn.

"Very good, smith. Lady Emmeline will thank you for it."

He nodded. "Then I am well pleased."

Without looking her way, Lance turned and left the hall, silently thanking Lady Idalia for her assistance.

If only he could thank her properly, he would gladly do so.

5

Though Idalia had been holding her mother's hand for some time, sitting beside her bed in the wooden visitor's chair, her mother had not awoken or even stirred. Idalia had begun to fall asleep herself, exhausted from the feast the day before, when a slight squeeze of her hand forced her eyes open.

"You appear tired," her mother said, her voice cracking. She tilted her head toward the sole window in the chamber. "'Tis evening."

Idalia wasn't sure how her mother knew since the sole window in the room was nearly always shuttered at her request. The light hurt her eyes, making the pain in her head worse.

"Aye, Mother."

Still holding her mother's hand, Idalia reached over to pick up the remarkable iron bracelet that sat on the table next to her mother's bed.

"A gift for the lady of Stanton," she said.

Her mother took it with her free hand.

"From?"

"The new smith. An offering for the Gule of August."

She watched as her mother turned it over in her hand.

"What is the engraving?"

Twisted in the center with two flat pieces on each end, it was as beautiful a piece as Idalia had ever seen. "It looks like a circle to me."

She'd been tempted to ask the one man who knew for certain, but it did not seem a good enough reason to visit the forge. While it was true she'd spent quite a bit of time there when Roland was alive, Master Lance was not Roland. And if her father had disapproved of her visits before, he would certainly do so now.

She hadn't realized her mother was watching her.

They'd looked quite a bit alike once, but her mother's illness had taken a harsh toll. When the whites of the countess's eyes had begun to take on a yellow tint, the physician had suggested they consult a priest.

"I'm sorry to have missed the feast." She handed the bracelet back to her. "Your father must have been surprised by his offering."

Idalia nodded. "Indeed." She placed the bracelet back on the table.

"What is he like, the new smith?"

She grasped her mother's frail hand once again. There was a time, not long ago, these pains came and went, naught but an inconvenience. A time when her grip had still been firm and strong.

That time had passed.

"He is . . ."

Handsome. Intense. He makes my heart feel like it's dropping down to my stomach every time I see him.

"Kind."

Idalia squirmed in the wooden chair as her mother watched her.

"Kind?"

"Aye."

"Hmmm."

Her mother's watchful eyes finally closed. If at all possible, she looked worse today than she had the day before. Fear thrummed inside her. "Marina will be along soon with food . . ."

When her mother shook her head, she took on the commanding tone she'd learned from the very woman who now lay before her.

"Mother, you *will* eat something."

Another murmur as her breathing slowed and she drifted off to sleep. Though Idalia hated how often her mother slept, she knew it brought her much-needed relief. Squeezing her mother's hand once more, she went in search of the lady's maid and found her returning from the kitchens.

Nearly the same age as the countess, Marina had served Stanton since before Idalia was born. Her dark hair was now sprinkled with gray, though it was difficult to see under the head covering she always wore.

"She's asleep again," she told the plump maid. "Please force her to eat something."

"I will try."

Together, they walked through the buttery, which connected the kitchens to the great hall. Barrels of drink surrounded them, the stone walls keeping the chamber cool. "The stores of wine are low," she commented as they walked through.

It was true. Idalia had planned to speak with a new wine merchant on market day. The last shipment they'd received had included too many bottles that had gone sour. They could not afford the waste.

"I will speak with Dawson in the morning."

"Very good. Now off for some rest yourself, my lady."

With that, Marina shuffled off into the hall, disappearing along the back wall, which led to the lord and lady's chamber.

It had been a long few days, but Idalia wasn't quite ready to retire for the evening. She wandered out into the courtyard without stopping to find a torch. The full moon provided enough light to illuminate her path to the Small Tower.

Though the courtyard was mostly empty by now, guardsmen passed through, preparing for their night watch. Just as she was about to unlock the door securing the tower, a chicken ran by, chased by a child she didn't recognize. Idalia knew most everyone who lived within the castle walls, so she briefly considered following the boy to question him.

The promise of a few moments of quiet beckoned, however, and she made her way up to the wall-walk. Once at the top, she took a deep breath, watching as lights diminished in the village below, one by one.

"A most unusual tower."

She spun around at the voice—deep, rich, and familiar—not having heard anyone behind her.

Immediately Idalia's heart began to thud, so quickly she wondered if he could hear it.

"Good eve, Master—"

"Just Lance, if it pleases you."

Lance. She'd begun to use the given name in her head, but to do so aloud . . .

"You followed me."

"I did. You left the door unlocked."

She nearly blurted out another question, one she had no right to ask. But from his clean trewes and linen shirt and still-damp hair, Idalia wondered if he'd been to the public bathhouse in the village or somehow managed to secure a private bath.

Why had such a thought even passed through her mind? Her older sister had always been the boldest of the three sisters, though sometimes Idalia thought Tilly might not be far behind.

"Why?" she asked.

"I imagined the view would be better up here than down in the courtyard."

By now her heartbeat should have returned to normal.

It had not even slowed.

"And is it?" she pressed.

He walked past her, close enough for her to catch his scent. She could smell dried woodruff and decided he must have somehow arranged for a private bath. It was not a common fragrance here in Stanton, but the scent was most pleasing.

As was the man himself. He stood shoulder to shoulder with her now, or would have if he weren't so much taller. In reality, it was more like shoulder to upper arm.

"What is that, in the distance?" he asked, pointing.

Idalia, accustomed to the torchlight where there should be none, smiled in anticipation of the tale she was about to tell.

"The spirits of Eller's Green dwell there."

She wasn't surprised he looked skeptical.

Pretending, as best she could, that her heart wasn't still racing as fast as her sister Tilly fled from her duties around the keep, Idalia explained, "We Northerners, as you know, are a superstitious lot."

"I know it well," he said, his lips tilting up slightly, although it could not quite be called a smile. "A good friend of mine, a Scot, takes a coin with him into every battle, believing he would otherwise be killed. He found it after his first battle, lying on the ground with no bodies close by or indication of where it had come from. Having been spared in the bloody altercation, Terric sees his coin as a sign. I fear for him to lose it, not because I think it protects him but because Terric truly believes it has special powers."

She smiled, understanding completely. Nodding to the light, she said, "None know why the wooded area there is called Eller's Green, but it's been so named for generations. Stanton Castle was granted to my great-grandfather, and according to those who know the tale best, the spirits were out there long before that."

She nearly laughed at his dubious expression.

"The lord of Stanton was returning home from battle when he dismounted his horse right there." She pointed just beyond the tower, to a thickly wooded area close to the source of the light. "Just beyond those trees."

The noises of the day had abated, and the quiet struck Idalia, reminding her she was very much alone with this handsome man.

"Some say he'd already been injured in battle. Others deny it. But all agree that when he fell to the ground, dead, it was the spirits who'd caused his death."

Lance stepped away from the battlement and leaned against the wall of the tower behind them, crossing his arms.

"They were angry at him, I assume?"

Of course he did not believe her. In truth, although Idalia found the story entertaining, she did not believe it either. But many did, as evidenced by the light peeking through the trees.

"Aye, for going to battle with his neighbor, a man many considered honorable."

She pointed to the light. "A small watchtower was built by his son. To this day, Eller's Green is never left unguarded."

That managed to surprise him, she could tell. "That light is a guard's torch?"

"Aye."

Lance shook his head. "Seems a waste of a man to me."

"To pacify the people who very much believe the spirits may return? Mayhap. Mayhap not."

She did look him fully in the eyes then, and wished she hadn't. Lance's face was nothing less than perfection. His brooding stare did nothing to slow down her heartbeat, which had again begun to beat most abnormally.

"Do you believe in evil spirits?"

"Nay," she admitted. "I do not."

"So what, Lady Idalia of Stanton, do you believe in?"

6

He should never have followed her.

Nor should he be asking Lady Idalia such questions, but he found himself drawn to her, unable to get her out of his mind.

The fact that she'd visited the forge, twice, told him she was different than most noblewomen, who would never dare to risk a gown that way. But that wasn't the only thing that drove him to her.

Lance had spoken to several people these past days in his quest to gauge the lord's interest in the order's cause, and in so doing, he'd learned quite a bit about the man's daughter. Not just that she'd assumed her mother's responsibilities, but that she excelled at them.

Kind. Compassionate. Nurturing.

These were the words he'd heard used most often, and from what he could tell, they rang true.

Beautiful. Haunting.

Those were the words *he* would use, if asked, about the woman who had inadvertently distracted him from his mission.

"Love."

It took him a moment to realize it was her response to the question he'd so boldly asked. She believed in *love*.

At times, he thought her timid. But she could be as bold as Guy, who tended to say and do as he pleased, consequences be damned.

"Love," he repeated, looking back out at that speck of light beyond the outer curtain walls.

"You don't agree?"

"They are your beliefs, and not for me to agree or disagree with."

A better answer than "no." There was no place in his life for love. Not anymore. It was a dangerous emotion anyway.

"They say women like me cannot marry for love," she said, her voice sadder than he would like it to be. "But both my mother and sister defied such a sentiment."

It was the first time she'd mentioned her mother.

"Your parents married for love?" He turned toward her again, trying hard not to dip his gaze down to the creamy pale skin of her neck, and below, which beckoned to him in the darkness.

"Of sorts."

It appeared that was all she intended to say on the matter, and Lance would not push her.

"So," she said, peering into his eyes, "if not love, or evil spirits, what do *you* believe in . . . Lance?"

He liked his name spilling from her lips.

More than he should.

He could not answer her honestly. To speak the truth would be to reveal himself in a way he could not. Instead, he found himself saying, "I believe if you were found here, alone with a blacksmith, there would be much for us both to answer to."

She only shrugged. "My father does not concern himself in the affairs of women."

"Surely he does so of his daughters?"

"He is a busy man. And while certainly he cares for my reputation, his focus is on 'keeping the people of Stanton safe,'" she said, quoting her father.

"A noble cause." And one that could either work for or against the Order, depending on what he decided would most benefit his people.

Idalia sighed. "Aye."

He sensed a sadness about her when she spoke of her father. Although Lance did not know the Earl of Stanton, he'd met many men like him. In some ways, Idalia's father and Conrad weren't dissimilar—both felt the keen responsibility of keeping their land free from those who would seize it, whether they be neighbors, distant relatives, or even the king.

By now, nearly all of the activity in the courtyard below them had ceased. Hidden behind the tower as they were, they were tucked out of sight of the sole guard in their area.

They were alone.

With that knowledge, a vision assaulted him of the gentle lady of Stanton, her hair unbound, as he reached behind her neck and pulled her toward him for a kiss. His body's immediate reaction forced him to remind himself this was no common maid.

Neither was she just any noblewoman. Lady Idalia was the daughter of the man whose support they needed if this rebellion would come to pass.

"I'm sure he is a finer father than my own."

Lance had not meant to blurt out such a sentiment. He'd meant only to alleviate his discomfort. But there it was.

"Oh?"

The details were ones he'd not share. With her, or with anyone. Even the Order. Only Guy knew the full story, and Lance had always wondered if his friend thought less of him because of it.

"We should go . . ."

"Lance." She stopped him with her hand, the featherlight touch scorching his arm. He wanted to seize it, use it to pin her against the stone wall.

"I do not know you well"—she pulled her hand away—"but I don't wish for you to think ill of my father. He is a good man. A noble leader. I believe as you come to know him and the people of Stanton, you will be glad to have come here."

For reasons that had nothing to do with his purpose, he admitted, "I already am."

☙❧

IDALIA WOKE ABRUPTLY, HER EYES FLUTTERING TO the sound of a door bursting open. She sat up, startled, wondering why her maid was staring at her so strangely.

"Apologies, my lady," Leana said. "I did not realize you were still abed."

Confused, Idalia looked at the light shining through the cracks in the window's shutters. The sun was up already. And she was not.

"Have I missed mass?" she asked as her maid turned to leave.

"Aye, my lady."

Leana, who was her exact same age of twenty and two, had resided at Stanton her whole life. Her father, Stanton's cook, had fled Scotland with his bride, who had been forbidden to marry an Englishman.

Tall and as bright and cheerful as her blonde hair, her maid could make the most hardened warrior smile.

"I'm awake." She swung her legs over the side of the bed, signaling Leana should return.

Washing with the rose-scented water Leana had brought with her, she watched as the maid shook out a pale yellow day gown.

"Was my absence noticed?"

Leana's pointed look was the only answer she needed.

If she'd missed mass, she'd also neglected to oversee the morning meal following mass. Dawson could just as easily have fulfilled that duty, but her father liked to go over castle accounts each morning immediately after mass. He never broke his fast with them, preferring to eat, and work, in private. There were times she did not see her father all day, and though he did typically attend the evening meal, he had been missing more and more of those as of late.

Since the priest had arrived and declared the countess's illness spiritual in nature, he seemed to be hiding himself away more often than usual.

"I don't know what overcame me," she said, removing her shift and stepping into the gown.

Another look. Though she'd asked Leana many, many times to voice her opinions without being asked, the maid still refused to do so.

"Leana?"

She slipped her hands into the arms of the gown, its sleeves fashionably low-hanging, but not so much so she would be unable to perform the many tasks required of her that day.

"'Tis your body speaking to you." Leana tied the laces at her back. "Since Roysa left, you have been doing all of the tasks she and your mother once did. Give more of the work to Dawson."

"Dawson more often angers our tenants than pacifies them."

Leana did not answer, for she knew it to be true. Dealing with Stanton's tenants, from keeping their homes in good repair to sorting out complaints, just was not the seneschal's specialty. He was efficient and quite intelligent, but his brusque manner did not lend itself to certain tasks.

"My mother would say that to ignore the signs of the body—"

"Is to ignore the life it possesses," she finished. "Aye, I've heard her say as much many times."

"And yet . . ."

"And yet, there is no one else," she said, meeting Leana's eyes over her shoulder.

That wasn't precisely true. She did enjoy the tasks she undertook on behalf of her mother, but there were so very many of them. Besides, as Leana finished lacing her gown, it struck her that there was another reason for her late morn.

Lance.

She'd forgotten the dream until now.

Instead of following him down the winding stairs of the Small Tower last eve, she'd grabbed his arm to stop him once again. He'd turned, looked at her as if asking permission, and kissed her.

Moving to the bed in a stupor, Idalia sat and lifted her feet as Leana slipped on her leather shoes. Her mind lingered on that imagined kiss. It struck her that she'd experienced more joy in the thought of kissing the blacksmith than she had in the actual event of kissing the man she'd been briefly betrothed to marry.

The son of a baron, Sir Christopher had visited Stanton more than once, their betrothal contract signed not long after Roysa's. On his last visit to Stanton, he'd pulled her into a private alcove on the ground floor of the keep and kissed her.

She'd later described the kiss to Leana as "pleasant." After all, her intended was handsome, the kind of man she should have been thrilled to wed.

When their betrothal was broken less than a sennight later, when their fathers had an argument that could not be resolved, Idalia's lack of feeling on the matter worried both of her sisters. Perhaps this was the reason.

"My lady?"

She hadn't noticed Leana watching her. Heat crept up her neck and settled in her cheeks. Though she looked at her questioningly, Idalia knew she could not tell the maid her thoughts.

Or could she?

Idalia considered Leana a dear friend and trusted her as much as she did her sisters. They shared both a thirst for knowledge that motivated them to learn about the world outside of Stanton—and a commitment to making Stanton Castle a comfortable home for all who lived there. Both women, as borderers, knew how quickly everything could be lost. Although Idalia's own father never spoke to her of such things, thinking them inappropriate to discuss with a woman, let alone his daughter, she knew as much as he did about Stanton's affairs. Luckily, neither her mother nor Dawson were so tight-lipped about their precarious situation.

Idalia shuddered.

And looked at her maid. Her friend. The only confidant she had left, really, with Roysa gone and her mother so ill. This was not a topic for Tilly's ears.

Sitting back down, Idalia clasped her fingers together on her lap.

"You can never tell anyone of this."

Leana's eyes widened.

"Promise me."

"You know I'd not speak out of turn."

Should she really say it aloud?

"The new blacksmith." Idalia waited, hoping her friend would discern her meaning and she would not have to continue.

But Leana simply looked at her.

"You saw him, in the hall on the Gule of August?"

Leana shook her head. "I was in the kitchens with father and missed the presentation of the gifts."

Though Leana was not a kitchen maid, she often helped her father as needed.

"You've not seen him, then?"

Confused, Leana shook her head. "Nay. But what does he . . . ?" Her mouth formed an *O*.

Neither of the women had much experience with men. Leana had been promised to a boy from the village, but he'd been killed in a border raid more than three years earlier. Her father was eager to find her another match, much as Idalia's father sought to find her a husband now that Roysa was married.

Neither woman cared to marry a man they did not love, although they both knew—Idalia, in particular—it was a battle they were destined to lose. Eventually, as the daughter of an earl, she would be wed to whomever her father chose.

"He is handsome, then?"

She thought of the figure he'd cut the night before as they stood side by side on the wall-walk.

"Very handsome."

"Lord Steffinshire's son was handsome too," Leana said, "but I do not remember such a blush on your face."

Another of her suitors. Leana was right, the baron's son had indeed been handsome—but he was no Lance Wayland of Marwood.

"I want to see him!" Leana squealed. She fairly ran to the opposite side of Idalia's chamber and grabbed the used water bowl and cloth. "I will meet you in the courtyard."

"Wait!"

Her maid was nearly out of the room before she was able to stop her.

"We cannot just go to the forge now because you want to meet him."

Leana's look said just the opposite.

"I have much to do this morn . . ."

"All of which will be waiting for you when we return."

Her heart sped up at the possibility of seeing him again, which was all the more reason to say no.

"We've no reason to go there," she hedged.

"Do we need one?" Leana asked, arching her brow. "We'll tell him the truth: I was sorry to have missed his offering and asked to be introduced to him. What did he give your father?"

"An iron bracelet. For mother."

Although Leana didn't comment, she didn't need to—the friends knew each other well enough for the words to go unsaid. The gesture had been thoughtful. Kind. And also perceptive.

Still.

"I cannot—" she began.

"Then I will go to him myself."

With that, the maid walked out, leaving Idalia scrambling to catch up with her. For she knew Leana well and had little desire to imagine what reason she might give the blacksmith for her visit. Though she doubted Leana would reveal her interest, Idalia would not chance such a thing.

Whether she liked it or not, it seemed the first order of the day would be to call on Lance. And if she were being honest with herself, she liked that idea very much.

$$\mathscr{X} \quad 7 \quad \mathscr{X}$$

"That's enough," Lance said to Daryon. The boy stopped blasting the bellows as Lance thrust the metal into the bright orange fire. He worked without thinking, hammering the metal over and over again until it cooled.

This was the last time it would be heated. The knives had been commissioned by Stanton's marshal, and thus far he'd made more than twenty of them. Placing the finished knife off to the side to cool, Lance took off his gloves and told the boys to get a drink.

It was essential in this heat to remember to do so, a lesson his father had taught him early and repeated often. Pushing away the thought, he considered instead a conversation from earlier in the morning. Lance had taken mass, even though it was not usually his custom, hoping it would help foster more of a connection with the people of Stanton. He'd sat beside one of Stanton's men-at-arms, and the man's conversation with the knight beside him had been of interest.

"It will not be long before taxes are raised again," the man had said to his friend—a common complaint.

However, the unpopularity of King John's taxes

46

was not necessarily an indication their lord would welcome a mutiny against the man. Still, Lance had listened to their conversation with interest.

"For a war we cannot win," said the first man.

"Cannot win? It's already been lost."

A justified argument. The Battle of Bouvines had been a disaster. As had each of his previous attempts to wage war with France.

English kings had long neglected the concerns of the border lords, but this king may have overstepped.

Taxes had never been higher. The methods of collecting them, never more ruthless. And the money was all being drained not for the betterment of the kingdom but for seemingly endless wars with France. With the latest loss across the seas, Conrad felt the time for action was upon them.

But to revolt against a king, more than their four-men order would be needed.

"Master Lance."

He'd been so deep in thought, Lance had somehow missed the flash of color at his door.

"Good morn, my lady." Daryon bowed handsomely to Lady Idalia and the woman at her side, whom he'd not yet met.

"You can join your brother," he told Daryon, who had stayed to work the bellows, the extra rush of air needed to keep the forge sufficiently hot. Miles had gone to the collier to fetch a supply of charcoal.

Wiping his hands on a cloth used for that purpose, Lance nodded to the women, indicating he would join them outside. As always, it took a moment for his eyes to adjust to the sun. He'd become accustomed to the darkness of the forge, but still . . .

It seemed just a bit brighter today, although he was admittedly not looking into the sky. Lance's gaze was firmly on the vision standing just opposite him. The collar and sleeves of Idalia's

CECELIA MECCA

yellow kirtle were lined in gold fabric. With low-hanging sleeves and a high neckline, the gown showed little skin, leaving the rest to his imagination.

One that had been too active of late.

"I'm pleased to introduce my lady's maid, Leana Adley."

"Adley," he repeated, tearing his gaze away from her to address the maid. She was lovely, and the fact that her beauty moved him not at all told him again how much he admired the lady of Stanton.

"Aye, same as the cook. My father," she said.

"Well met, Mistress Leana."

"I regret not having been in the hall for the presentation of gifts at the Gule of August feast. My lady told me of the beautiful bracelet you gifted her mother."

She was well-spoken for a cook's daughter. She'd no doubt lived among nobles her whole life. As Idalia's maid?

"It was my honor to create the piece for her."

He returned his attention to Lady Idalia. "I trust you are well this morn, my lady?"

"Very well."

That smile could chase away his demons, of which he had many.

"As often as my lady visited Roland, I've not come down here often," Leana said, peering into the forge. "You are young for a master blacksmith."

"Leana!"

He reassured Lady Idalia he wasn't offended. "I apprenticed under my father," he told the maid, "and spent the last few years as the master smith to Lord Bohun."

"Bohun," she repeated, rubbing her chin. "A border lord?"

"Aye."

48

"We are certainly lucky to have you at Stanton. Roland was much loved here—"

"Leana . . ." Lady Idalia cleared her throat.

"Apologies, Master Lance. It seems my manners have fled somewhere this morning."

He didn't understand the look she gave her lady, but something told him the maid was most certainly up to something.

"Oh dear, I nearly forgot. I was to assist my father this morn. One of the kitchen maids took ill. My apologies," she said, turning to flee up the hill.

She was gone in a moment, her blonde braid bouncing in her haste to leave.

Lance stared after her.

"Your maid is . . ."

Lady Idalia crossed her arms, also staring at the empty spot where Leana had been a moment ago.

"Incorrigible."

Her fond tone belied the word she'd chosen. Obviously she cared very much for the woman who'd just been swallowed up by Stanton's great courtyard.

"I am sorry for the interruption. You are engaged in your work."

"Nay," he said.

Much, much too quickly.

It was true, he had another ten knives to make. But he didn't want her to leave just yet.

"Daryon and Miles have gone for supplies."

It was unlike him to struggle for words, but it was also unlike him to knowingly court disaster. He knew no good could come from speaking with Stanton's daughter. From looking at her. From longing for her.

Not when he wasn't willing to use her for information.

The night before, he'd decided he'd shun any additional conversation with Idalia, but that decision had been made when not in her presence. With her standing here, just steps away, he found he was simply not ready to part with her just yet.

Since the natural landscape separated the forge from Stanton's other buildings, most of which were scattered throughout the courtyard above them, it was easy to spot the lone figure watching them from above. When Lady Idalia saw him, she turned, sighing heavily.

"Father Sica," she explained. The man finally moved on, although Lance wondered how long he'd been standing there.

"I do not care much for the priest." Immediately clasping a hand over her mouth, she amended, "He is a man of God, of course. And so deeply revered by me and all of Stanton."

Her cheeks had turned an eye-pleasing pink.

To quell her mortification, he admitted, "I do not care for him either."

Her eyes widened. "You've met him, then?"

"Nay, but I've taken mass."

She looked down. "I missed mass this morn."

"Something that is not typical for you," he guessed.

"No."

Lance wasn't expecting what he saw when she looked back at him.

She looked embarrassed, but why? He'd already admitted he disliked the priest as much as she did, so he doubted this was over missing mass. And something about that look, and the way her eyes lingered on his arms . . .

I should not ask.

"Tell me," he blurted out, knowing it was foolish to do so.

But she didn't need to say a word. Her lips parted. The hue of her pink cheeks deepened.

"You did not sleep well."

She shook her head.

"Nor did I," he admitted, his eyes still on her. He allowed his meaning to flow into the words. "Lady Idalia."

"Idalia, if it pleases you."

Naught would please him more, but he could not. She was the daughter of an earl. Of *this* earl.

"It would please me very much to have leave to use your given name, but—"

"Then do so."

He swallowed.

"*Lance.*"

She was both timid and bold—a mystery he should like to solve. But he could never forget he was here for a purpose. And that purpose was not to anger the earl by becoming too familiar with his daughter.

His young apprentices bounded toward them, wagon in tow. They would be upon them any moment.

"Idalia," he said, despite knowing he should not, and then he made it much, much worse.

"Can you meet me again this eve?"

He didn't say where. Or when.

But she knew, and nodded.

She grabbed her skirts and turned from him, meeting the boys midway up the hill. He watched her greet them and eventually disappear.

What the hell did I just do?

✣ 8 ✣

"**H**e is a whoreson," Idalia's father muttered under his breath. Their guest had arrived just before supper. She didn't recognize him, but according to Dawson, he was the son of a border clan chief. As such, he was seated with them at the high table. She'd been forced to distract Tilly from the epithets constantly streaming from her father's mouth, all spoken just loudly enough for both of his daughters to hear.

She was accustomed to his language, of course. But he reserved the worst of it for the very man their guest now praised—the Scottish king who would only allow Stanton's wool across the nonexistent border in exchange for what amounted to an expensive bribe.

"I would not disparage the English king here in your hall," the man was saying, "but his policies do not make it any easier for us to trade either."

Idalia smiled politely as the young man caught her eye—and then she turned away.

"I do wish Mother were here now." Tilly pushed the vegetables on her trencher back and forth. "She had a way of containing Father's language."

"Has," Idalia chided gently. "Has a way. Mother will get better."

Tilly did not look convinced. If only she truly believed her words, Idalia might do a better job of making her sister believe them too.

"She is getting worse."

Indeed, she was. Marina had said she'd refused to eat today, a more common occurrence of late.

"Oh, but I was to tell you she took a bit of bread and cheese earlier."

"When? Marina told me she hadn't eaten."

"Just before supper. You were in the kitchens when she found father to tell him so." Tilly lowered her voice. "So that is good, is it not?"

"Aye," she reassured her.

Tilly glanced over Idalia's shoulder and leaned closer, lowering to a whisper. "Father Sica was here when she told us. He and Father argued about it."

"As they seem to do more each day."

The priest was becoming more and more insistent that he be allowed to "treat" her mother. So far, he had been denied. No one else believed her ailment was a punishment from God or that she may be possessed by the devil.

"He cannot be allowed to see her," she said.

"Mmmm." Tilly was already thinking of something else. Idalia could always tell when her mind wandered.

"What are you thinking?" Idalia lifted the goblet of wine in front of her and brought the sweet liquid to her lips.

"I worry for you at times."

She looked away, not wanting to meet Tilly's eyes just then, and realized she was being watched by their guest. Straightening, she nodded to him and asked, "Is the meal to your liking, my lord?"

Not wishing to talk any longer about her mother —or to think about the meeting she'd arranged for after dinner—Idalia conversed with their guest and her father until the two finally rose, signaling the end of the meal.

Heart pounding, she carried about her normal activities, inquiring after the other guests in the hall— various retainers and tradesmen—and visited her mother as she did each night. She then retired to freshen up, using the rose water Leana always left out for her. She was just about to leave when it occurred to her exactly what she was doing.

Preparing for her assignation.

With the blacksmith.

That she was meeting him, alone, should have been reason enough to give Idalia pause. Lance was not a man to trifle with. Although he was kind and honorable, there was a darkness in him. Besides which, even the most rational part of her knew nothing could come of their friendship.

The thought of how her father would respond to the notion of a match between his daughter and the blacksmith nearly made her laugh aloud. He'd slam his mug on the table. And once he overcame his sheer disbelief at her audacity, he'd utter every swear word he'd ever learned.

So why am I meeting him? Father Sica already saw you together.

Unlatching the door, pleased that few moved through the courtyard at this time, Idalia left the wooden door unlocked behind her and made her way to the exact same spot where she and Lance had spoken the night before.

She stopped abruptly when she saw he was already waiting for her at the top of the Small Tower.

He turned and Idalia barely stopped herself from gasping at the sight of him.

He looked no different than earlier in the day, though cleaner of course. But something in his expression . . .

Lance knew what she did. That this attraction between them had no place in either of their lives. And yet, here they both were.

"How did you get up here?" She'd left the door unlocked, assuming he would have to follow her up.

Lance held out a small iron circlet with a lone key hanging from it.

"I am a blacksmith" was his only answer.

"And a good one if you were able to replicate the key so easily."

He rarely smiled, which was likely for the best—the effect was devastating. It was a smile meant to tease, not necessarily to taunt.

"Roland was not nearly as skilled," she said honestly, joining him along the outer battlements.

"My first master . . ."

"Your father," she clarified, noticing his reluctance to speak of him as such.

"Aye, my father. He served King Henry, and his own master was considered one of the most skilled blacksmiths in all of England at the time."

"And so he passed those lessons down to you."

Lance didn't answer.

When she glanced at his profile, Idalia was not surprised to see his tight-set jaw, and though she knew the topic was one he did not wish to discuss, curiosity forced her to press him.

"You do not care for your father."

His breathing grew noticeably heavier, making Idalia immediately regret the question.

"I am sorry."

"You've no need to apologize, my lady."

"My lady?"

"Idalia," he clarified, and the familiarity of her name coming from his lips made her very core clench in anticipation.

Anticipation? Nay, never that.

"It was an impertinent question."

He did this thing then, with his tongue, that Idalia had seen him do before. Not a licking of his lips precisely, but for a moment she spied his tongue as he wet first the top and then the bottom lip.

She was staring.

"Nay," he said, "I do not like my father."

Even though she'd suspected as much, to hear him say it so bluntly . . .

Her own father could also be quite difficult at times. And as her mother became more and more ill, he was getting worse. But she liked him, of course. Loved him dearly.

How could a father push away his son so effectively?

"Yet he taught you many things?"

"Aye."

He would say no more on the matter, so she tried a different topic.

"And your mother?"

Lance closed his eyes, and Idalia silently cursed at herself for having chosen poorly.

"She is no longer with us," he said, his voice soft.

Idalia's heart sank. "I am so very sorry."

She was filled with the desire to reach out and touch him. His hand, his cheek. Anything that might offer comfort. Of course, she resisted the urge.

To touch him would be to give in to this madness consuming them both.

"Two years after I left Marwood, I received word she was ill. By the time I arrived home . . ."

Idalia thought of her own mother lying, even now, in her bed as she'd done for nearly a sennight. The pain hadn't lifted this time.

"Now it is I who must apologize." He turned to her. "I did not mean to make you worry about your own mother."

"Nay," she said, forcing her voice to be strong. "Mother will recover, of that I have no doubt."

Telling herself the same, over and over and over again, made the visits to her mother's sickbed more tolerable. It hurt to see the mother she'd always looked up to, who'd always been such a vibrant force of nature, brought so low.

"I'm glad to hear it."

He was looking at her, a question in his eyes, and something about that look urged her to unburden herself. Who better to speak to than a newcomer to Stanton?

"Around the time of the last harvest, mother began getting pains here." She pointed to the side of her head. The moon afforded them ample light to see each other, although his face was cast in shadow. "They came and went, but each month, they seemed to be getting worse. The physician gave her skull-cap, which alleviated them for a while. And then . . ."

She looked up toward the keep, her eyes finding the part of the keep where she knew her mother would be lying, asleep.

"The pain in her head moved downward, to her stomach. She is resisting eating this week, and the whites of her eyes are tinged with yellow."

Idalia could not bear to think of them. Her eyes, Father Sica claimed, were evidence of the devil's work. "In fact, these last few days they appear more yellow than white."

There. She'd said it.

Lance ran a hand through his hair. "That does sound unusual."

"If word spreads of mother's condition," she continued. "My father fears my sister and I will not make a good match if Father Sica's thoughts on the matter are spread."

Idalia looked toward Eller's Green. "If there are bad spirits, certainly there must be good ones too?"

Lance moved to stand directly next to her. So close. She didn't step away, but at least she forced herself not to do as she wished and move closer.

"Some would say you speak of the saints. Of God."

"Some?"

He didn't answer, but neither did she press him.

"We should not be here," he said, his tone flat.

"Nay, we should not."

Idalia looked down at his hand, where the key still hung from his hastily made circlet, then asked, "Does that mean we will not meet again?"

She wished to take the words back even as part of her was proud for asking the question. It had been uncommonly bold of her.

"Would you like to meet again?"

She did not hesitate. "Aye."

"Then we shall. Tomorrow evening?"

Her heart soared. "Tomorrow evening."

Lance bowed deeply. More deeply than her station warranted.

"Until then, my lady."

She felt the loss immediately as he walked away. When Lance stopped just before entering the tower, she thought for a moment he'd changed his mind and would stay.

"Idalia," he corrected.

This time, she did not mistake his tone. More than familiar, it dripped with promise and longing, and if she could summon the nerve to utter his name aloud, Idalia was pretty sure hers would do the same.

Which would not do at all.

9

L ance handed Daryon the punch and nodded.
"I've not used it before."

His brother, the more self-assured of the two boys, had just stepped outside. Which was exactly why Lance had given Daryon the tool now. Although Miles did not intend to hold his brother back, his skills sometimes intimidated the more soft-spoken lad.

"I know you haven't, lad."

Lance stepped aside. "Make sure it's hot enough," he said, watching as Daryon put on his gloves and used the pliers to heat the end of the horseshoe. When the iron glowed, he placed it back onto the forge, picked up the punch, and looked up at Lance with wide eyes.

"Now turn it and use the pritchel hole to punch the backside," he said, even though Daryon already knew what to do. If he could say one good thing about his father, it was that he'd never assumed Lance could do something he'd never tried before. Watching and doing were two different things.

"That's it," he encouraged as the boy created the first of six holes that would be needed. He worked quickly and efficiently before the shoe cooled.

He did it easily enough.

"You're doing a fine job."

"He has a fine mentor."

He spun toward the door, leaving his apprentice, and embraced the man who strode toward him.

"What are you doing here?"

Guy released him and nodded toward Daryon, who was now cooling his handiwork in a bath of water. He understood. It wouldn't do to talk openly in front of the boy.

Guy approached the boy, who'd set down his tools, hand outstretched.

The mercenary could be both brash and callous, but he could act the part of a gentleman when he so chose.

Taking off his glove, the boy stuck his hand out tentatively.

"You are a lucky boy," Guy said to the bewildered apprentice. "Your master is the most sought-after smith in all of England."

Daryon's eyes widened to the size of coins.

"Truly? All of England?"

"And Scotland too," Guy boasted.

Lance rolled his eyes, though neither of them noticed.

"I've even heard them speak of him in France, so coveted is his work."

"Daryon," Lance interrupted. "Go find your brother. I will finish up in here."

The boy looked down at the shoe. The expression in his eyes spoke of a certain longing.

"We'll be sure to show Miles tomorrow before giving them over to the marshal," he said, reading the boy's thoughts.

The boy grinned at him before scampering out of the forge. The door nearly always remained open to allow sunlight in and smoke out, but Lance shut it behind Daryon as he automatically began to clean the shop.

"You're earlier than expected," he noted.

They'd agreed it would take Lance at least a sennight to gather the information they needed, perhaps more.

"I'm impatient."

"I have little information yet."

Guy leaned against the only semiclean surface in the shop, the stone wall behind him. "We have Baron Chauncey."

Lance whistled. The East Anglian landowner was both the itinerant justice on the eastern circuit and sheriff of Norfolk and Suffolk. Unlike Stanton, he was unusually vocal with his grievances against the king. Most expected his tenure as the king's servant to end at any moment.

But for now, he was a powerful ally, and not one Lance would have expected the order to secure so soon.

"Conrad managed it?"

Guy nodded. "He spoke to him just after you left."

"The baron will be discreet?"

"Our treason is his own."

A typical Guy answer. For as many years as the two had known each other, Lance still had a difficult time gaining direct answers from his friend.

"And how have you fared?"

Each of them had support to gather. That his role was as important as the others left Lance more humbled than he'd shared with the men.

"I've not seen Terric since the tournament," he said of their friend whose role was nothing less than gaining the support of the king of Scotland. "But Fitzwalter is ours."

"So quickly?"

Guy's smile was his only answer. All knew Robert

Fitzwalter had a personal reason to dislike the king, but that Guy was able to secure him to their cause so quickly was still surprising.

"Stanton?" Guy asked.

Moving toward the only open window with a clear view of the path leading to the forge, Lance adjusted the shutters—leaving them open only a crack so he could spy the path—and turned back to his friend.

"I'm still not sure where his loyalties lie. The people here have yet to embrace me. That the previous blacksmith here was beloved by all hasn't helped my cause."

Guy snickered. "Your dour disposition is unlikely to have helped."

Lance cocked his head to the side. "If only we could all be as pleasant as you."

They both knew the description hardly fit. While it was true Guy smiled more easily, those who knew him would not use the word "pleasant" to describe him.

Confident. Witty, sometimes cuttingly so.

But not "pleasant."

"What have you learned?"

With a glance through the crack in the shutters, he thought about the conversations he'd had in the past few days.

"Two of the king's men were housed at Stanton when I arrived."

Guy groaned.

"But I don't believe the welcome they were given goes beyond simple hospitality. I've been listening, and while none of the people here are openly hostile, the general sentiment seems to align with our own."

"Have you spoken to the earl?"

"Briefly." Lance glanced through the gap in the shutters again. The sun was beginning to set, each minute bringing him closer to his arranged meeting with Idalia.

Guy watched him.

"You're withholding something."

As soon as his friend had arrived, Lance had known his connection with Idalia could remain a secret no longer. Guy was the type to ask uncomfortable questions. Always had been.

"I presented him with a gift during their Gule of August feast. I learned nothing of import."

Guy only looked at him with a raised brow, his meaning obvious. He was not about to stand down unless Lance told him all.

"I have spoken to his daughter," he admitted.

"And what have you learned from her?"

Lance kept his expression neutral. "That her mother, the countess, is extremely ill. 'Twas Lady Idalia who suggested I bring a gift for her father on the feast day."

"And?"

He sighed. "Nothing more, although the gift was well received."

Still, Guy waited.

"I am meeting her on the battlements after supper," he said as clearly as if his mouth were filled with porridge.

And, of course, got the exact reaction he had feared.

"Pardon?" Guy leaned forward. "It sounded as if you said you were meeting the earl's daughter in some private place at a preordained time this evening."

Lance ground his teeth.

"I presume you've spoken to the woman on other occasions?"

He remained silent, which was confirmation enough.

"How old is the earl's daughter?"

"The same age we were when we met." Of course, Guy had not asked *which* daughter. And Lady Tilly was likely around ten and three or ten and four.

Guy's eyes narrowed. "Does he have more than one daughter?"

Lance tried not to smile, something not normally a problem for him given that smiling hadn't come easily to him since he was a young boy.

"Aye."

"By the blood of Christ, Lance."

He conceded finally. "His eldest daughter is married and gone. The middle one, Lady Idalia, is a few years younger than I am, mayhap twenty and two? And aye, before you ask, she is quite comely." He paused, then added, "In answer to the other question you have not yet asked, I will not use my relations with her for our cause."

Guy's ever-present grin faltered.

"Think about this carefully."

"I have. And will not do it."

Lance had thought of little else since the night before. The earl depended on his daughter, more than he realized, and she would be a powerful ally. But he refused to manipulate the lady, especially given the trust she'd shown him.

On this, he would not waver.

"You do understand the importance of this mission?"

"You expect me to answer that?"

He wasn't angry, exactly. Lance could understand his friend's position.

"You could make this easier than we ever expected," Guy said.

Lance moved to open the door. "We eat in the hall."

He left Guy behind, not waiting for the footsteps he heard moments later. "Are you staying the night?"

Catching up to him, Guy made a grunt of assent as they circled around the forge to the small two-room building that was Lance's new home.

"I'm off to wash in the stream just outside the gate, but you're welcome to wait here."

Before his friend could press him on Idalia any further, he walked away, the echo of Guy's curses following him.

He wasn't coming.

Idalia looked down at her hands, clasped together in front of her. Despite the unfashionableness of her gown, she liked not having to pull back low-hanging sleeves. Her sister Roysa shook her head every time Idalia wore it, or a similar gown.

Despite Roysa's ability to make her feel small with naught but a look, Idalia missed her terribly. Roysa, like her mother, always knew what to say. How to act. Who to tend to first. She'd been raised as the eldest. And Tilly, the youngest.

Idalia was ever the middle child—the one who was sometimes forgotten—although she'd never much cared about that. As long as her family was safe and content, she was happy. She'd never wanted anything else, or even thought to want anything else.

Until now.

The steadfast nature of her emotions, a quality her father had always admired, seemed to have abandoned her of late. Or, more specifically, since Lance had come to Stanton.

Knowing it was wrong did not make her thoughts of him go away. Instead, she found herself conjuring his face all day. Sitting with her mother, who seemed a bit better today thankfully, Idalia had sworn to herself she would not think of him once. Her mother deserved more than a wayward daughter who did naught but daydream about a man she could never have.

But he'd refused to leave her thoughts.

Her mother, of course, had noticed her distraction. Idalia had insisted it was naught but the weight of acting as the lady of Stanton. Since she'd missed the last market day, they were low on both grain and wine, and it would fall to her to resolve the problem.

And yet, her disquiet came from an altogether different source.

Idalia was falling for the smith.

Which, of course, was not very practical. Nearly every day since Roysa's wedding, she'd expected her father to make an announcement about a new betrothal. If not for her mother's illness, Idalia did not doubt she'd already be married or nearly so.

And yet, here she was, waiting for Lance.

It was well past the time they'd met the night before. Which was really just as well—she should not be here anyway. No matter what she wished, this meeting could serve no real purpose. Perhaps he had come to the same conclusion.

With a final glance at the specks of orange and yellow light moving to and fro in the village, Idalia turned away.

And gasped.

"I did not even hear you approach."

Her heart began to beat wildly, much like it had the night before, as she took in Lance's casual attire. His shirtsleeves were rolled to his elbows, and the low-hanging top gave more than a glimpse of the sculpted chest beneath. And though it was covered now, she thought of the mark on his upper arm. And of the muscles beneath it.

"You were leaving."

No emotion. No judgement. Just a simple statement.

"Aye. I thought perhaps you'd changed your mind."

Idalia had never, ever wanted to be touched by someone this badly before. They stood within touching distance, and she could not help but imagine his hand reaching out, making contact with her skin. She licked her lips, realized she'd done so, and tried, unsuccessfully, to catch her breath.

"I have a visitor."

He didn't move, and neither did she.

"Oh?"

"A friend."

"A friend," she repeated, waiting for more. Then, remembering he was a man of few words, she prompted him further. "What is your friend's name?"

"Guy." He blinked. "Guy Lavallis."

"Is he a smith also?"

The way he was looking at her made Idalia shift her weight from one foot to the other. She wanted to crawl out of her own skin. Impatient for . . . something.

Nay, for *him*. To know his touch. Lance kept his thoughts and emotions to himself—she'd quickly realized that much—but she wanted to know them. To know him. She wanted to get closer to him.

"He is a mercenary."

"Oh."

She wasn't sure what to say to that. Idalia had never met a mercenary before. Stanton had no use of them, but certainly she'd heard of such men.

"For?"

"For whomever pays him the most coin."

Idalia swallowed, berating herself for asking. "I see."

"We met at the Tournament of the North many years ago, when we were both boys."

She had questions, but Lance did not seem inclined to offer many answers.

"Are you always so . . . ?" She struggled to find the right word.

"Reticent?" he provided with a glimmer of amusement.

"Aye." She supposed it would do.

"Most often, yes."

"You don't have any siblings, do you?"

"How did you guess?"

She smiled, imagining Roysa standing there with them now. "You would not have been allowed to say so few words with sisters around."

He actually smiled. "I could have brothers."

"But you do not."

"Nay, I do not."

"I have no real notion of who you are, Lance Wayland." Indeed, the facts she'd collected were thin. All she knew of his past was that he'd trained under a father he disliked, lost his mother, and had no siblings. Now he was here at Stanton, where people shunned him for not being Roland. But she hoarded those few facts as if they were gold coins—and she wanted more.

When he took another step closer, Idalia knew something was about to happen.

Nay, not something. More than *something*.

And she was as powerless to stop it as she was to heal her mother. Or make her father notice she was more than a glorified steward.

So she stood there, immobile. Attempting to breathe like a normal person.

"What do you want to know?"

Her eyes raised to his lips.

"That, my lady, will get us both into trouble."

She looked up. "That?"

"Aye. *That.*"

She did know, of course, to what he was referring. Idalia glanced over to where the guard would be standing, but he was out of view from where they stood behind the tower's entrance.

"Idalia . . ."

Lance's shoulders rose and fell.

That will get us into trouble.

He was right.

Idalia turned back toward the battlements only to be spun back around. Two firm hands guided her face toward him. And, just like that, his lips were on hers.

She kissed him back, his lips so soft and warm.

He pulled back abruptly.

"You've not kissed a man before."

"I . . . I have."

His hand still cupped her face.

Lance brought her toward him once again. This time, with a hair's breadth between them, he said, "Don't be scared."

"Scared?"

When he touched her this time, she closed her eyes. And nearly jumped when she felt his tongue gliding along the crease between her lips. Opening them just slightly, Idalia startled to realize his tongue was still there. She touched hers to his, not sure if that was right.

It certainly *felt* right.

His mouth slanted across hers, showing her what to do next.

She followed his lead, becoming bolder as his hands moved from her face to the back of her head. He pulled her closer, and when she responded by wrapping her arms around his shoulders, the sound that came from deep within him shook her to her very core.

It was a sound of pleasure. Of longing.

He desired her.

That thought, coupled with what he was doing to her mouth, enveloped Idalia in a way she'd never experienced before. She wanted to be even closer, surrounded by this man in every way. And she must have communicated that with her lips, because he pulled her toward him.

She let her fingers rest on the nape of his neck as his mouth slanted over hers.

When he pulled away, she licked her lips instinctively, wanting to taste where he had just been.

"You learn quickly."

Though he didn't let go, Lance looked in the direction of the guard. They were still hidden, though in truth, Idalia should be more worried about being discovered.

Instead, she wished to know how Lance felt about what had just happened.

"My tutor said the same."

His brows raised. "Tutor, aye?"

A laugh welled inside her chest and escaped in a most unusual sound. Almost as if it were a giggle. But Idalia did not giggle. That was usually the purview of her younger sister.

"You know very well what kind of tutor I meant."

He looked at her lips, and Idalia nearly blurted out the question.

Will you kiss me again?

"I enjoyed that very much."

"As much as the other kisses?"

"The other . . ." Then she remembered telling him she had been kissed before. "They were nothing like that."

He leaned down, opening her mouth as he'd done before. This time, she knew immediately what to do and matched his tongue's caresses with her own.

When a loud clang from below them rang out, she pulled away.

But not out of his arms.

"Likely," he said, loosening his grip just slightly, "because an earl's daughter should not be kissed that way. At least not by someone other than her husband."

"How sorrowful that is."

When he laughed, Idalia's chest swelled with happiness. It was such a rare sound from him, and all the more treasured for it.

"You should laugh more often."

"You should kiss more often."

Her smile felt wide enough to split her face in two.

"You believe so? I wonder, will anyone else be willing to instruct me?" She pretended to think. "I've no suitors currently, but—"

"I meant me."

Of course he had. But Idalia took immeasurable joy in teasing this man who'd obviously had so little lightness in his life.

"Oh dear, I did not realize."

He stopped her with another kiss, and this time, he did not coax her mouth open. This time, he silently demanded it as soon as their lips touched.

She complied most willingly. The sensation of his tongue touching hers as his lips moved over her own . . . she was pretty sure this was the most pleasant thing she'd ever experienced in her life.

Idalia never wanted it to end.

But it did.

"Surely you'll be missed soon?" Lance said, pulling away although he looked reluctant to do so.

"Not at this time. Come morning, always."

He reached up to a lock of her hair that had fallen forward.

"You are the lady of Stanton in your mother's stead."

Lance twirled the hair between his fingers.

"Aye."

"But you do not mind it."

She looked at her hair between his fingers out of the corner of her eye. It seemed such an intimate thing for him to do. But surely not as intimate as the kisses they shared.

"Nay. It makes me happy to see Stanton thrive. If it were not for Mother . . ."

He dropped her hair then, but she smiled when his hand returned to her waist to join the other.

"Tell me of her."

She thought not of the woman lying in bed, but of the mother who had raised her and her sisters. The woman who'd always been so full of life.

"She is the most remarkable woman in the world. Kind. Full of joy and love for all. If she has any faults, I don't know of them. Everyone is a better person with her near."

Lance looked at her curiously.

"You do not believe me?"

"Nay, 'tis not that. I believe you all too well. But wonder if you speak of your mother or someone else?"

"What do you mean?" she asked, her brow furrowing.

The look in his eyes was her answer. He was telling her that she'd described her own qualities.

"I have many faults," she argued.

"Name one."

"Weakness. You are not my husband, yet here I am, standing in your arms. Wishing you would kiss me again."

He did, but it was only a short kiss this time.

73

When he pulled away, he sighed and said, "I would argue we are all weak to some extent."

"Even you?"

"Especially me."

Lance stepped away from her then, and she felt the loss immediately.

"Does that mean we can meet again?"

His gaze never wavered.

"If you were caught with me . . ."

"You're worried for your position here," she said, her voice flat. By his expression, Idalia knew her guess was correct. "I would never betray you."

Lance sighed heavily, looking at her with a combination of longing and regret. His shoulders sagged. "It was wrong of me to come here tonight. You are Lady Idalia—"

"Nay. I am simply Idalia."

"And I am nothing more than a smith."

She wanted to argue with him. But he was, indeed, a blacksmith. A man she could never be with for more than a few stolen moments. He left her with a sad smile and the knowledge that her passion had been awakened, and dampened, all in one night.

❧ 11 ❦

"**I** am not your damn apprentice," Guy said, but as he did so he tossed Lance a pair of pliers.

Catching them, Lance winked at his actual apprentices, both of whom giggled at his friend's joke. Guy had spent the day with them in the forge. Yesterday, he'd done the same. The distraction had helped Lance stay away from Idalia, although it had done nothing to stop him from thinking about her. He doubted if anything could.

"Go ahead," he told the boys. Darkness had already fallen, and it was time for them to go home.

Guy watched the brothers leave. "Good boys, those two. Like we once were."

Lance didn't flinch, although he knew at once what Guy spoke of. He was convinced Guy simply liked to argue. Why else would he have brought up the incident again, all these years later?

"But would you call our actions 'good'?"

"Yes." Lance started cleaning the shop as he spoke. Not willing to be dragged into one of Guy's mental meanderings—the man could talk for hours without reaching a resolution—he changed the topic. "How long do you plan to stay at Stanton?"

He'd been here for two days, and while Lance was

genuinely glad to see his friend, Guy's presence had not helped him make connections with the people here. Everything about Guy was . . . grand. His looks. His gestures. The mercenary had made it his life's work to attract attention—something that usually helped him find a new master willing to pay for his services.

Which was exactly why Lance had attempted to keep him contained in the forge. Lance's goal wasn't to attract attention here at Stanton—he needed to blend in, to become one of them. It was the only way anyone would dare lower their guard around him. The only way they might admit to entertaining a hint of opposition against the king. Only then could he gauge if Idalia's father might be receptive to them.

Idalia's father.

When had the Earl of Stanton become Idalia's father?

Two nights ago when you kissed her, that's when.

"You're thinking of the girl again."

"Hardly a girl," he said, tossing his apron onto the stool.

"If you allowed me into the hall again, I might observe her better myself and form an opinion."

He rolled his eyes. "Exactly the reason we don't venture there."

Guy crossed his arms. "You want to be rid of me, do you not?"

"Aye." He didn't bother hiding what his friend already knew.

"And I want to appease my curiosity before I go. The only woman to ever catch the eye of Lancelin Wayland of Marwood. She must be a beauty indeed."

"You'll not meet her." He'd kept his friend within sight at all times to ensure it.

Guy sat next to the dying flames, the forge's fire nearly extinguished for the night.

"You forget our purpose," Lance muttered.

"*I* forget our purpose? You have an intimate encounter with a woman who can give you direct access to the very man whose support we need, and *I* forget my purpose?"

He should never have told him, but Guy could be persuasive, and apparently Lance did not hide his feelings well. An oddity, that—he'd always thought he was an expert at that particular talent. When he'd come back from meeting Idalia two nights ago, Lance had not intended to share anything with his friend.

But he'd confessed all in the end, and had been paying the price since.

"We've been through this . . ."

"Aye, and you're still in the wrong of it. But this is your mission, not mine. I've brought my man to our cause, and now you must do the same."

"My mission," he grumbled. "You'd do well to remember that."

Guy ignored his warning. "If only we could eat a real meal this eve."

He would live to regret this.

"You'll remember, my goal here is to assimilate. Not bring attention."

Guy bounded up from the stool, clearly sensing weakness. "As you will." He placed a hand on his stomach. "A right fine meal. I look forward to it." He made to leave the shop.

"Say nothing."

"My specialty," Guy called back from the doorway.

His friend's specialty was wreaking havoc wherever he went. But if he were being honest with himself, Lance wanted to see Idalia.

Even though he should not.

No good could come from making an appearance in the hall, especially with Guy, but he would take the

CECELIA MECCA

excuse anyway. Just for a glimpse. He wouldn't speak to her, but one quick look might help ease his tortured soul.

One he knew, if given the chance, Idalia could heal.

❦

"YOU'VE DONE WELL, DAUGHTER."

Idalia was indulging herself in a quick glance at Lance, who had come into the hall earlier with his friend.

"Pardon?" she asked her father.

He rarely praised her, and Idalia did not know what to think of it. While the words were welcome, they appeared to be somewhat forced.

Which could only mean one thing—it wasn't his own sentiment.

"You've been with Mother?"

Her father raised his chin as he often did when he did not want to answer a question. Tilly snickered beside her, having evidently heard the entire exchange.

"Aye. When did Lord Sheely arrive?"

"Earlier today," she said. "Dawson told him you were not available, so he appealed to me for an audience."

Although they rarely turned away a visitor, not all were equally welcome. Especially one who had come to collect the king's coin. It was no secret her father despised Lord Sheely. And since their neighbor to the south had been made royal tax collector, he had become even more insufferable than usual. His visit was yet another reminder that the king's taxes had become a heavier burden for them to bear.

Her father grunted.

"You will not be able to avoid him for much

longer," she said, resisting the urge to look toward the back of the hall.

"I can attempt it," he muttered, making her smile just slightly.

"Is it true," she asked, taking a spoonful of soup, "he keeps a portion of the coin he collects?"

Dawson had told her that this afternoon, after they'd shown Lord Sheely to one of the empty chambers. But the seneschal was also known to tell tall tales and gossip.

"Aye." Her father took a swig of ale, a cue he was finished speaking on the topic. So she turned to Tilly instead.

But not before taking another glance at *him*.

He was watching her.

"You have an odd look about you," Tilly said.

She looked away immediately, her eyes landing on her sister.

"I don't."

"Aye, you do."

She would not bicker with her sister in front of their guests and retainers. Especially since Tilly was likely correct. In the past few days, *everything* had felt odd.

Before, she'd been content to move about her daily routine.

But that was before Lance.

Before his kisses.

Before the longing looks he was giving her, which seemed to say he regretted their decision as much as she did.

Stop. Looking.

"I spoke to the physician this morning," she said to both her father and sister, hoping to distract Tilly, and herself, from the reason Idalia could hardly form a coherent thought.

"The physician is glad she's eating but worries her condition does not seem to be improving."

"His worries are not helping her heal," her father said, his tone edged with frustration. "'Tis good I sent for another physician from London."

"Nay, they are not. I am glad of it as well."

"And there are whispers again." It was Tilly who'd spoken, and Idalia and her father both turned to her in surprise.

"I slipped into the bakery before supper and heard him speaking of . . ." Her sister stopped and made a face. Idalia could guess the reason.

"Father Sica?"

"Aye. Apparently he told Cook, who told a kitchen maid—"

"Tilly," her father warned.

He hated that her sister involved herself in gossip. But no matter how often Tilly was told to refrain from such matters, she continued to do just the opposite. Her mother and father had gotten into many disagreements about her sister's "wayward" behavior, but none of it seemed to affect her.

Tilly was . . . unique. And Idalia loved her for it.

"I will speak to him." Her father raised his mug to the captain of the men-at arms, the gesture telling them both, in no uncertain terms, he was finished speaking on the matter.

Which left her to . . .

No. Don't look.

She looked.

Lance was speaking to the other men at his table, who seemed to be slowly accepting the new smith. Which reminded her to speak to the hayward. He had influence with the others and could be persuaded to give the smith a chance to find his footing at Stanton.

He may not need her help, but Idalia could not

resist the urge to help him. Being alone in a new place could not be easy, especially when the old smith had essentially been part of their family.

Lance met her eyes and held them, his expression serious.

He smiled so little. Why?

Unbidden, she thought of his lips on hers, slanting for complete access, which she'd so willingly given him. It was as if some other woman had stood upon those ramparts with him. Certainly Idalia would not have allowed such liberties.

Aye, it was you. And you enjoyed every moment of it.

As the meal ended, she assumed he would leave with the others. But with more than half of the hall already cleared, both Lance and his friend remained.

"Confound Sheely," her father muttered suddenly, his tone too soft to be heard farther down the table. "Have you heard his blathering? He's more than halfway up John's arse, but . . ."

He cut himself off.

It was the kind of comment he'd have made to her mother. She suspected he'd forgotten his daughter sat beside him and that his wife lay asleep in her sickbed. Her father stood, joined by everyone else in the hall, including his daughters.

The meal was now officially over.

Tilly wasted no time bounding up from her seat, off to their mother's chamber. Idalia normally sat with Mother midday until preparations for the evening meal demanded her attention, and despite Father's protestations that they must leave their mother to sleep, Tilly enjoyed crawling into her bed in the evening. Which left Idalia to walk among their retainers, listening to informal complaints and even a kind word every so often.

Still, as she made her rounds from table to table, he stayed.

Before long, she had been to every table but his. Avoiding it would seem unnatural.

Attending to it, disastrous.

But she had no choice.

"Good eve," she said, approaching. Only four men remained, including Lance and the mercenary. Idalia concentrated on the others until she was forced to give the smith her attention.

"I do not believe I've had the pleasure of an introduction," she said as the mercenary stood.

"Sir Guy Lavallis of Cradney Wrens, my lady."

"May I present," Lance said, standing as well, "Lady Idalia, daughter to the Earl of Stanton." Though he'd finished with the introduction, it almost seemed as if he had more to say.

"Sir?" she blurted out without thinking, forcing her gaze back to the mercenary. "La . . . Master Lance mentioned you'd arrived here a few short days ago at Stanton. I do hope your stay has been a pleasurable one."

"It has, my lady. And made more pleasurable this eve, if I may be so bold to say so."

Ah, she knew his kind well. This was the kind of man accustomed to taking whatever he wanted. A handsome rogue. Hair that appeared dark now but not so much it would remain that way in the sun. Full brows and lips, which lifted slightly now. But his sweetened words had no effect on her. Roysa, had she not been wed, would have fallen for the handsome man in a trice. Which was no disrespect to her sister. Roysa herself admitted to being smitten with rogues.

Idalia had different taste.

Lance was looking at her, eyes hooded. She wished she could remind him that he had been the one to put distance between them.

Because right now, he looked as if he wanted anything but.

Idalia's pulse raced at the thought of being alone with him again.

"May I compliment you on the beauty of Stanton Castle?" Sir Guy said.

"I would be pleased to show it to you." Doing so was one of her favorite duties, one she'd gladly assumed from Dawson. Idalia was quite proud of what her family had managed to accomplish with the Anglo-Saxon structure.

"It is well lit," she rushed to explain, "so there's no reason to wait for morning. My day is often taken up with many other duties . . ."

The mercenary stepped away from the trestle table. "We would be most honored to tour the keep now." He looked at Lance, who definitely did not look honored.

In fact, he appeared to want to throttle his friend. The interest and desire with which he'd regarded her earlier in the night was nowhere to be seen. Perhaps she'd imagined it.

Idalia ignored that uncomfortable thought, excused herself, and spoke to one of the maids to arrange for her to assist Cook in the kitchen's cleaning. Rejoining them, she could not help but notice the difference between the men. Lance scowled. Sir Guy—a knight, which she would not have guessed—grinned like a squire who had just been given praise by his master.

"This," she said, addressing Sir Guy, "is the great hall of Stanton Castle, although you've obviously surmised as much already."

The tour would be simple. Ignore Lance. Pretend she was not hurt by his rejection. Distract herself by interacting with his friend. She would hardly even remember he existed.

❧ 12 ❧

Frustration coiled in Lance's stomach. His shoulders tensed. Every time she looked at him, he envisioned hauling her against him, continuing where they'd left off two nights before.

There was much he would love to teach her.

As Idalia showed Guy about the keep, she spoke only to him. And his friend's easy grins did nothing to alleviate Lance's rapidly deteriorating humor.

"This is one of the only private areas in the keep," she said, bringing them into a small chamber on the ground floor. "It was once the chapel, before the other was built more than twenty years ago."

"Why is it so well lit, being abandoned?" Guy asked.

He'd wondered the same but didn't trust himself to speak.

"My lady," a voice interrupted from the door. The maid looked as if she'd run through the entirety of the keep. "I was told you might have come this way. Pardon for disturbing you, but the leg seems to be broken on one of the tables in the great hall. It's been carried away but needs repair before morn."

"Did you speak to Dawson?"

The seneschal seemed a nice enough man, but he

certainly was not the one maintaining Stanton in the countess's absence.

"Aye, 'twas he who sent me to find you."

"Our woodworker has been ill these last few days," she explained to them. Well, mostly to Guy.

"I can assist," Guy offered. "I was once employed by a woodworker in France. A foul man, if truth be told, but skilled nonetheless."

Why a woodworker would have use for a mercenary, Lance could only guess. He'd not heard that story before.

The maid looked at Idalia, who nodded.

An idea bloomed, and Lance spoke before he could decide against it. "Guy is capable in many areas," he said, eliciting a smirk from his friend that thankfully neither of the women noticed. "I have no doubt he'll fix your table if you would continue the tour." As he finished, he caught Idalia's gaze at last.

Her eyes narrowed.

Guy scowled.

The maid simply stood there, hands folded, waiting for assistance.

"Show me the table." Guy's tone was nearly brimming with admonishment, but Lance didn't—and couldn't—care just now. He wanted to be alone with Idalia to ask her the reason for her animosity toward him this night.

As if he didn't already know.

"This way, sir," the maid said, still seemingly unaware of the undercurrents in the room. As she led Guy away, he glimpsed a very brief change in Idalia's expression.

A crack that he meant to exploit.

She's not a damn castle, Lance. She is a woman. A beautiful, kind, and very sensuous woman.

"Was that wise?" She did not move from her position as Lance shut the door behind the maid. They stood some distance from each other, candles flickering all around them.

Though it no longer served as a chapel, the remnants of a stone altar stood beside them. Otherwise, it was now nothing more than an empty chamber with more wall torches and candles than he'd ever seen in one space.

He decided to be honest.

"Likely not."

She frowned. A rare expression, and one he felt ashamed to have elicited.

He was as good for her as he'd been for his mother. Which was why he turned to leave.

"Wait."

Only a monster would ignore the vulnerability in her voice.

And he was no monster. For all his faults, Lance was *not* his father.

"I . . ."

He turned back, understanding. She wanted to be alone with him as much as he wished to be alone with her. But wanting did not make a thing possible.

"Why did you stay?"

Goddammit.

Why did she have to ask such a simple, logical question?

"I'm sorry about that night. I should never have kissed you."

It was as blatant a lie as he'd ever told.

"Then why did you?"

"Idalia," he started, and then stopped. This was more dangerous than she realized.

"Tell me," she demanded as if she'd been raised to make demands and have them honored.

Because she had. His lady was an earl's daughter. She practically ran Stanton Castle.

"Never in my short life have I wanted to kiss a woman more than I did that night. Than I do now."

Lance forgot to be cautious as he moved toward her.

"More than that, I would like nothing more than to lay you down on that altar, strip you of every bit of clothing, and show you much, much more than a simple kiss."

He stood so close now Lance could smell the unique scent of citrus blossom that was Lady Idalia of Stanton.

"What," she asked, swallowing, "would you show me?"

The combination of curiosity and fear in her tone, in her gaze, told him she knew this was wrong. It was madness, really. But she asked, so he answered.

"I would show you every song your body is capable of singing. I would show you what it means to die the little death and come back to life. I would show you all of me."

That last bit, he'd not meant to say.

But it was true. For once, Lance wanted to share himself with someone. Somehow, he knew she'd not judge him for the sins he'd committed.

"I would like that," she said simply.

Lance shook his head. "As would I. But we cannot."

His actions and words were at odds, and Lance knew it well. For even as he continued to shake his head in denial of what could not be, he reached for her.

She came to him, and melded with him as if she belonged there.

Capturing her mouth, Lance immediately slanted for better access. He simply could not get enough of her, the kiss quickly spiraling out of control as he spun them around so her back was against the old altar.

And then he did something utterly mad.

Staring at her low neckline all night, he'd dreamed of this . . . although he had not imagined it would actually happen. Particularly not in an old chapel.

He feathered kisses down her long, swanlike neck, which she arced toward him as she grasped his arms. His cock strained, fully erect. Flicking his tongue as he moved lower, he gripped the stone behind her to restrain himself.

It did not work.

Groaning, he pulled the material of her gown down. Lower, and lower still, just enough.

The sight of a bare breast nearly unmanned him. Perfectly round, the nipple so much darker than he'd imagined. Without looking up, he lavished it with the same attention as he had her neck, first circling the taut center, then taking it fully into his mouth.

Lance wasn't sure when her hands had moved to his head, but they had, and she was pressing him even closer. So he pushed just a bit further, using his teeth to test. When she gasped, he did it again.

And then he made the mistake of looking up.

Eyes hooded, lips in a full pout, Idalia was the final course of the most resplendent meal, and he planned to indulge.

They had to stop.

Covering her on both sides, he stood to tell her just that.

But Idalia was not having it.

"No, not this time."

He looked toward the door. While this area of the keep may be unused, private, they were taking an impossible risk. "They could come back any moment."

"Aye."

He was almost disappointed she'd agreed with him.

"Or they could not. But I don't want you to stop."

"Idalia, I—"

"Show me."

Oh God, no. Please, no . . .

"You know we cannot. You are an earl's daughter."

Not *an* earl. *The* earl.

But he'd awoken something in her. Her chest heaved with unspent desire. She ached for pleasure, and he wished to be the one to give it to her. To be the first to show her the satisfaction a man and woman could find in each other.

You are risking . . . everything.

Damned if he cared at this moment.

"What are you wearing under your shift?"

That managed to surprise her.

"Under my shift?"

"Aye."

The woman whose bare breasts were still exposed to his mouth actually blushed. What could possibly make her . . .

"You've nothing under it?" he guessed.

She shook her head. "Socking on my lower legs of course, but naught else. Roysa chided me for it, but—"

"Do not be embarrassed." He emphasized his next word. "Ever."

Idalia seemed to understand. With him, there was nothing to shy away from. Lance would never think ill of her. If she wanted to run naked through the courtyard, she should do so.

Maybe not that.

Such an act would certainly get him into trouble.

More trouble than what they were about to do?

Lance shook away the thought.

Responding to the look she gave him, and his own

desire to see Idalia's face the first time she was well and truly pleasured, Lance reached under her gown and shift. Where he should have felt hose, his hand found bare flesh instead. He didn't know which of them was more shocked. He'd caressed many bare legs before. But the feel of her soft flesh as he made his way toward his goal . . .

Groaning, he captured her lips once again. This time, she responded immediately and without reserve. Closer and closer until, "Open your legs a bit for me," he whispered.

Still no barrier.

It was so unexpected he actually paused for a moment before pulling back, wanting to see her expression.

Moving beyond the curls, which he'd dearly love to see, Lance dared her to tell him to stop. Instead, eyes wide, she opened those pink lips ever so slightly just as he reached her folds.

"Don't be afraid."

"I'm not."

Her quick response humbled him. Why did she trust him so?

She shouldn't.

Another unwanted thought Lance pushed aside.

He entered her with first one finger and then a second, her gown the only barrier between them as he moved, slowly at first. Though Lance dearly wished to take advantage of the fact that her lips were now parted wide, begging for a kiss, he refused to give into that temptation.

As he moved his fingers, his thumb circling just the right spot, her chest started rising and falling with greater intensity. His lady was breathing heavily, her cheeks flushed pink.

Lord, he would give everything, had he anything to give, to see such an expression every day of his life.

Her eyelashes fluttered prettily as a beautiful groan escaped her lips.

She was close.

"There are many ways for a woman," he said, "and a man to find pleasure. This . . ."

He slowed the pace and pulled away, ignoring his cock, which he dearly wished was inside her instead of his fingers. Even thinking it . . .

No. Stop.

"This is one way. All I need you to do now, Idalia"—her name was yet another caress—"is let your body relax."

Another quick rub with his thumb.

"Come for me, beautiful."

It was not simply an endearment. It was the truth.

And she listened.

The wetness against his fingers forced him to close his eyes, steady his breath. Damn if he wasn't as close to release as he'd ever been without a single touch.

When he opened his eyes, Lance wished he hadn't. She looked undone—a few strands of hair had escaped her braid, and her pink cheeks practically glowed in the candlelight, her eyes glistening above them.

"I would do that again, properly," he said without thinking.

"Properly?" Her voice was barely a whisper.

Lance kissed her then, his hand readjusting her gown as he did.

"You taste so damn pretty."

Idalia smiled. "I cannot *taste* pretty."

He disagreed.

Then, stepping back regretfully, he glanced toward the door. "If we'd been caught . . ."

"But we were not."

"I'd not have expected you to be so daring," Lance

said as he attempted to force his wayward cock back from the edge.

"I am not usually so," she admitted. "Lance?"

"Aye?" He took a final deep breath to steady himself.

"I would have you do that again."

She said it so casually that Lance couldn't help but smile, something he'd done much more than usual since meeting Idalia.

"I would do that, and more, if—"

They simultaneously turned to the door as it re-opened. Their time here, alone together, was at an end.

✣ 13 ✣

Thankfully, her mother had eaten earlier. But she did not look well at all. Her eyes still had a decidedly yellow tint, the same one Father Sica insisted was evidence of the devil's taint.

As they awaited the physician Father had sent for from London, Idalia's mother fluctuated between awareness and sleep. When her eyes popped open, Idalia breathed a sigh of relief. She secretly feared that one day her mother's eyes would simply remain closed.

"How long have you been sitting there?"

As her mother lifted herself to sitting, Idalia rearranged the pillows behind her head. In truth, she'd started her vigil at her mother's beside just after the midday meal. Idalia could not bring herself to leave even though there was much to be done.

But her mother disliked hearing that she or her sister had spent so much time in her bedchamber, so she lied.

"A short while."

Marina came in then with a washbowl. She approached the bed and came to a stop beside Idalia, who took the fabric from her hand and dipped it into the still-warm, rose-scented water.

Her mother hated to be doted on, attended to—for a countess who could have had servants to supply her every need, it had always been just Marina. And yet, she allowed Idalia to wash her anyway.

Avoiding her mother's eyes as she worked, Idalia wrung out the cloth and dipped it into the water again.

"Tell me."

Startled, she dropped the cloth into the water. Her mother typically reserved that tone for times when a firm hand was needed.

Picking the dripping cloth back up, she wrung it out once more. "Pardon?"

Her mother reached for her hand as she glided the cloth across her exposed arm, the sleeveless shift one of many her mother wore these days.

Her beautiful gowns sat unused in their storage chests.

"I do not know—"

"Tell me, Idalia. What troubles you?"

Even before the countess had fallen ill, some also whispered that she was a witch. An absurd claim, of course, but as much as the people of Stanton loved her, even Idalia could not deny her mother's ability to know what she shouldn't.

If the miller's wife was ill, her mother knew of it. When one of the kitchen maids was with child, her mother told the girl even before she realized it herself.

She knew . . . everything.

But, ill as she was, Idalia hadn't expected her to pick up on the fact that her daughter's world had changed forever, that her every thought was consumed by a certain smith. She'd not seen him all day. Thankfully, his friend Guy had not seen anything more untoward than two people standing precariously close to one another. But surely he suspected something.

Even now, the thought of seeing him at the evening meal . . .

"A man," her mother said, guessing.

She could not deny it. But could she admit to *which* man had captured her heart?

Idalia did not fear her mother would send Lance away. It was something her father might do if he ever discovered what was between them. But her mother? Nay.

But that didn't mean she'd condone such behavior. As Lance had said himself, she was the daughter of an earl. Her husband would be a man whose station could match, or elevate, her own.

"The blacksmith," Marina blurted out.

Idalia's mouth dropped open. She stared at the maid, shocked. "How . . . ?"

Had someone seen them coming, or leaving, from the Small Tower? Plenty of people spied her giving Lance and Guy a tour of the keep, but that was not such an unusual thing to do.

She realized her mistake at once—her reaction had confirmed Marina's words.

Her head whipped back to her mother, who was giving her an inscrutable look.

"The same one who forged that bracelet for me."

Idalia wanted to bolt up from the bed and run away. She didn't, of course, but the urge to do so was overwhelming.

"Aye." Her heart pounded as she waited for her mother's reaction.

The Countess of Stanton may be ill, but the fire in her eyes had not died. The woman who looked back at her was the same woman who'd commanded Stanton's men when Idalia was but six years old. The earl had ridden off to the Holy Land with the king, leaving Stanton in her capable hands. When a Scottish border lord laid siege to the castle, believing the earl's absence signaled the castle was ripe for the taking, Idalia's mother had stopped him.

"Bring him here," her mother said in that same commanding tone.

Bring him here?

"Mama, please do not dismiss him. Lance is a good man."

Her mother raised a hand, stopping her pleas. "Dismiss him? Has he done something that would warrant such an action?"

She pushed away the thought that had immediately popped into her head—Lance with his mouth on her breast and his hand under her skirts. "Nay."

"Then why would you believe I'd do such a thing?"

Idalia glanced back up at Marina, who simply shrugged.

Traitor.

"He . . . because he is a smith. And I—"

"Are a woman. We should have had this discussion much sooner. Especially now that Roysa is married."

Idalia groaned inside, though she did not dare to make such a sound out loud.

"Mother, please."

"I was married. Before your father."

Her hands stilled, the wet cloth hanging from them. Idalia searched her mother's face for any indication she was jesting, but those yellow-tinted eyes stared back at her, unwavering.

"You were married to another man?"

"It was many, many years ago. But aye, I married a man with whom I'd fallen in love. He was a warrior. The son of a Scottish reiver."

This could not be true.

"You were married to a . . . reiver? A Scot?"

Marina moved away as Idalia's mother spoke.

"We married in secret. My father did not approve." Her mother, already pale, appeared even more so now. She'd not met either of her grandparents, both of whom had died before she was born, but she'd heard of them, of course. Her grandfather had been a powerful border lord, an English baron whose title had passed on to Idalia's uncle.

But never had she heard a hint of this other man, this other husband. Did her father know? Her sisters? Nay, they would have said something.

"This was surely a scandal?"

Her mother's weak smile made it impossible for her to be angry at her for keeping such a secret.

"Very much so. When he died less than a year later in a raid . . ."

Her mother closed her eyes, and Idalia edged closer to her. She hated seeing her in pain, physical or the kind that came from the memory of lost love.

"I dare say my father was not pleased. And I never forgave him for his treatment of the man." She opened her eyes. "Much as he never forgave me for what I'd done."

"Does Father know?"

"He does. Our betrothal had already been pledged when he learned of it. My father said I was lucky such a man was still willing to marry me. No longer a virgin." She winked. Her mother actually winked.

Idalia's heart soared at the simple gesture. This was the charming, strong-willed woman she remembered.

"I came to love him, your father. As you well know. But in the beginning, I felt nothing but anger and resentment. It was a trying time for us all."

"You never told us." The bitter words slipped out.

"And I never planned to," her mother admitted. She looked tired now, her eyelids growing heavy again. Their conversation was coming to an end.

"Why do you tell me now?"

Lying back down, her mother closed her eyes. "Bring him to me," she muttered, bringing an end to their rather odd conversation.

The cloth now cold in her hands, Idalia watched her mother drift off to sleep. She turned to find Marina sitting near the fire, bowl in her lap.

The older woman did not look even a tiny bit repentant.

Idalia narrowed her eyes, attempting to give Marina the same withering look her mother could summon when displeased. But it must have failed because the impertinent maid chuckled. She actually laughed at her. Idalia may be doing her mother's job, but she was not her equal.

At least, not yet.

Then she thought of her mother's request.

Lance was not going to be pleased.

❧ 14 ❧

"What did you say?" Lance hoped he'd misheard her. It sounded as if the countess, lying sick in her bedchamber, wanted to see him.

He'd spent the meal attempting to avoid overtly staring at Idalia, knowing it would only remind Guy, who had decided to stay, of his indiscretion.

With the earl's daughter.

They'd barely finished their repast when he saw the flash of royal blue moving toward them—Idalia. Her father had never come to the hall for supper, but according to the men around them, such an occurrence was not unusual. He'd made fewer and fewer appearances since the countess had taken ill.

Idalia's expression confirmed he had heard her correctly. Her gaze shot to Guy, who'd taken a few steps away, giving them as much privacy as was possible in the hall, although he could clearly hear all that was being said.

"She guessed something was amiss. And inquired after the cause. How Marina knew, I'm still unsure. The cowardly maid ran off before I could get the full story, but it seems—"

"Idalia." Lance's tone was calm, assured. Not at all

what she'd been expecting, he could see. "You've done nothing wrong."

He meant every word—the last thing he wanted was for her to feel ashamed—but he didn't need the censorious look Guy was currently giving him to know he'd made a grave mistake.

If Lady Emmeline wished to speak to him about her daughter, this could very well be his last day as smith at Stanton Castle. Which would leave him with two choices. Asking the earl directly for his position on the king's policies, at the risk of being branded a traitor, or leave without the support they so desperately needed.

Neither option was desirable, and he deserved Guy's censure for having put himself—them—in this position.

"I do believe your friend thinks otherwise," Idalia said, glancing at Guy.

It was his turn to silently warn off the mercenary, not an easy task as Guy rarely backed down. But he did now, for her sake.

Ever the gentleman.

"Will you come with me?"

Dammit. This was not good. "Now?"

"Aye," she answered sheepishly. "My mother can be a tad impatient. She was resting when I left, but if I know her . . ."

She trailed off, leaving him with no choice but to comply.

"If you'll pardon him a moment," she said to Guy, who bowed in parting. "This way."

He followed her through torchlit hallways and up a circular stairwell at the back of the hall. As they climbed higher and higher, Lance realized he was in trouble for a different reason than he'd anticipated.

About to put the most important mission of his life in jeopardy, he could think of only one thing as the stairs beneath their feet gave way to a small empty corridor. Lance would like nothing more than to spin Idalia around and ensure she would remember him fondly if they were separated after this meeting.

Indeed, when she stopped and turned, he nearly gave into such folly. Her lips parted, and Lord if he would not like to kiss them.

"I am sorry," she said, unmoving.

"There is nothing to be sorry for."

He had no idea how close they were to her mother's chamber. Lance only knew, in this moment, they were alone.

Cursing himself, he nonetheless found himself reaching for her. Grasping the back of her neck, he pulled her toward him, taking full advantage of her acquiescence. In no time, the kiss spiraled from a quick joining to one that threatened to make him lose control.

What is wrong with me?

He pulled away, regrettably.

"I could not resist . . ."

"I'm glad for it," she whispered.

The way she said it told him he was not the only one who feared they might be parted. There was nothing for it, but the thought saddened him more than it should. More, even, than the possible failure of his mission.

"Come."

She spun away from him then, down the corridor and toward yet another stairwell. When they came to a door at the top of the tower, Lance took a deep breath. And followed Idalia inside.

The round chamber was dark, and despite the warmth outside, a fire roared in the hearth adjacent to one of the largest beds Lance had ever seen. Canopied, it took up an entire wall, making the lady who lay in it look absurdly small.

Her yellow-tinted eyes flew open and immediately sought him out.

Following Idalia closer to the countess, he watched as she pulled the coverlet down and sat up. She looked near identical to Idalia, although older and decidedly ill. Though her movements were slow, she did not appear frail in any way. But as they approached, he could see she was in pain. Wincing, she sat against pillows, which Idalia tenderly rearranged behind her head.

"Mother, may I present Lance Wayland of Marwood."

She nodded toward the woman who was so like her. "My mother, Lady Emmeline, Countess of Stanton."

He'd met few countesses in his time, and even fewer while standing above them in their beds. But Lance did know enough to bow deeply.

"Is my daughter a virgin still?"

Idalia made a strangled sound.

Though surprised at the countess's directness, he did not hesitate to answer. "She is, my lady."

"Mother!"

"I'd have asked you earlier," she addressed Idalia, "but I wanted to speak to the man who has stolen my daughter's heart."

Stolen her daughter's heart? Surely not. They hardly knew each other. And yet . . .

He had risked everything for a few stolen moments with Idalia. Did that not mean something?

"Mother, please—"

"I've little time for pleasantries," she said, pointedly ignoring Idalia, "as you can see. So I will ask directly. Are your intentions honorable, sir?"

Sir. She could not know that was an accurate moniker. Of sorts. None but his four friends knew

Lance had been knighted. Or of his true purpose here.

And even though she'd used the title solely as a courtesy, the reminder of his deception was an unwanted one.

Were his intentions honorable? He'd not expected or prepared for such a question.

"I have never acted dishonorably toward a woman in my lifetime," he said honestly. "And would not presume to do so now."

That much was true. Unless one counted it as dishonorable that he'd made this woman come apart in his hands, knowing he intended to sway her father to a cause that would put all of Stanton in danger.

Which, on second thought, maybe it *was* dishonorable.

"If we met in the hall, under different circumstances, I might ask you to leave Stanton Castle," the countess said, her gaze unwavering. "But we do not. I am dying—"

"Mother!" Her cheeks had turned a brighter pink than they had the other night.

"I am dying," she repeated. "And have married one daughter off to a man she does not love, even though she believes otherwise. But this one"—she never looked away—"will make her own choices. And I will be at peace with them if I can be assured you are worthy of such a treasure."

"Mother, please. We shared one kiss. That is to say . . ."

Lance would remember this moment for the rest of his life.

He did look away from the countess then, just in time to see Idalia purse her lips together in the most obvious expression of guilt imaginable. From the look of her, she didn't lie to her mother often—and she certainly wasn't very good at it. For all her passionate responses to him, Idalia was still an innocent. He would not smile, but damn if he didn't want to.

"We are not in love. And are certainly not getting married." She said it so adamantly Lance felt a pang at her words.

Of course they were not. Why should her refusal matter to him?

"I see," was the countess's only response to her daughter. "You will come back tomorrow," she said to him. "Idalia, will you send Marina to me?"

He caught Idalia's frown as he bowed once again, the encounter with her mother one of the strangest he'd ever experienced.

"I am so, so sorry," Idalia said as soon as they left the room. "I told her nothing except—"

He cut her off with a kiss.

Lance was acting reckless, but he needed just a small taste of her sweetness, her caring. In that chamber, she'd thought only of his feelings. Her mother's wellness.

Did she ever see to her own well-being?

He pulled away, wanting the answer to that question.

"Who cares for you, Idalia?"

She swallowed. "Cares for me?"

He stared at her lips, still wet from their kiss.

"You worry about offending your mother. And me. But what of yourself? Who worries for you?"

She was utterly perplexed by the question.

"I do not need anyone to worry for me."

He'd expected her to respond as such. It struck him then that they weren't in a private place. Anyone could come through this passageway at any time. "Is there anywhere more private that we can talk?"

"I have to find Marina. Meet me at the Small Tower?"

Lance didn't even bother arguing with himself about it. "Aye. I will be waiting for you."

Lady Idalia of Stanton was a woman worth waiting for but, despite what her mother had just said, was not, nor would ever be, his.

❧ 15 ❧

Idalia pushed her way into the Small Tower but did not ascend the circular steps in front of her. Instead, she leaned against the inside of the door, breathing heavily. She'd fairly run to find her mother's maid, and then here.

Was he waiting for her?

More importantly, what in the heavens had her mother just said to them?

Lance had reacted so calmly throughout the whole encounter. Indeed, he'd seemed almost amused when she'd stumbled over that small lie she'd told her mother. Idalia had not wanted to be dishonest, but what else could she have said? That he'd done something more wondrous with his fingers than she'd ever thought possible?

That she ached for him whenever they weren't together?

Idalia had even dreamed of him. That morning, Leana had remarked on the fact she'd awoken with a smile on her face. How could she not smile? The way he looked at her, and touched her, made her feel like the most beautiful and desirable woman in the world.

But he was troubled.

So much so that Idalia wanted nothing more than

to learn the cause. To heal the wounds he so obviously carried with him each day.

But . . . marriage?

Was it her mother's illness that caused her to say such things? She shoved aside the wicked thought that Father Sica might be right. The devil did not possess her mother.

And yet, she hardly knew the woman they'd spoken to earlier.

I'm dying.

It was not true. Idalia refused to believe it. But if her mother thought it to be true, she supposed such a sentiment could change the way a person thought of everything around them.

Taking a deep breath and climbing the stairs, Idalia opened the door at the top and saw him immediately.

When he turned, her breath caught. Her entire body felt as if it were a bowl of pudding, and for a long moment she could do naught but stand there looking at him, like a simpleton.

"I thought you may not come." His deep, resonant voice vibrated through her very soul.

"If anyone should be running for Eller's Green, it is you. After that discussion . . ."

She trailed off, not knowing what to say.

He did not move toward her. An awkwardness had settled between them after their audience with her mother, one she would do anything to dispel.

"I will admit, it was certainly not what I expected."

"What did you expect?"

"To be tossed from Stanton, at best."

The thought had occurred to her as well. To save his position and his reputation, she'd been prepared to promise she would never see or speak to him again.

A promise that would have killed her.

The thought sent a pang through her chest.

"I am sorry—"

One moment Idalia stood there, wishing there was not so much distance between them—the next, she was in his arms.

"Do not" was all he said as he held her.

She squeezed him, reveling in the feel of him in her arms, then turned to face the stars and settled back in his embrace, wishing she could stay this way forever.

Neither said anything for some time.

"Is your mother . . . is she truly dying?" he asked finally.

Her answer was instantaneous. "Nay."

He was quiet again.

"Tell me of *your* mother," she said finally, wishing to hear of the woman who had made such a man. Would that she could have known her. She squeezed him, as if to encourage him to speak, but he remained silent for a time. When he *did* finally speak, her heart jumped in her chest.

"She was so beautiful. Every man in the village whispered about her beauty. And caring, like you."

Idalia's heart hurt for the pain she heard in his voice. She was glad not to see his face. If she did, she might cry—something she did easily—and that wasn't what he needed from her just now.

"I don't speak of her often."

"Why?"

One hand moved to her head, and the simple act of Lance caressing her hair was, as of this moment, her favorite thing in the world.

"My father . . ."

His tone hardened. Instinctively, Idalia braced herself for his next words.

"He was a decent man, at times. His skills as a smith are renowned."

His words were heavy with sadness—or was it anger? Idalia could not tell which.

"But when he drank too much ale . . ."

His hand stopped moving through her hair. He slung it around her shoulder, linking his hands about her, and Idalia braced for his next words.

"He became a different person. Mean. Mocking."

This was difficult for him. His strained words made that abundantly clear. Wanting, needing, to see his face, she pulled away to look him in the eye. He let her. She encouraged him silently, and he kept going.

"He hit her. So many times. And I did nothing."

She would not cry.

"I pretended not to hear her cries. Hid outside at her bidding when he was at his worst. I was a coward."

"You were a child," she countered.

"I could have told someone, though half the village likely knew."

"And they'd have done nothing. She was his wife—"

"Exactly."

Lance had only ever looked at her with kindness, but there was no mistaking the hate in his eyes when he spoke of his father.

"Did he . . ." She swallowed but forced herself to finish. "Did he kill her?"

His bitter laugh was a sound Idalia never wanted to hear again.

"Nay. But he might as well have. He made her life miserable." He'd been looking above her, off into the distance somewhere, but his eyes lowered to hers. "I was ten and five the night I finally struck back."

Idalia did not look away.

"Still an apprentice, still young, but strong. Nearly as strong as my father."

She thought of the muscles in his arms, formed, no doubt, from years of wielding a smith's hammer, and could only imagine the same was true of his father.

"I'd resolved not to let him touch my mother ever again. There were stretches of months he did not drink. Occasions when he slept in the forge. But I knew it would happen again, and it did. He came home one night smelling of gut-rot, and I knew the time had come."

Idalia shivered, scared. Though she did not know for whom.

"He'd not expected me to stop him. When I grabbed him from behind, he was stunned at first. I struck him with all of the anger I felt toward him, and despite his size, I knocked him right to the ground." Lance closed his eyes. "Mother screamed the entire time. Yelled for me to stop, that he would hurt me." He opened his eyes again. "But he did not. He lay there, holding his jaw. Stunned."

She would not cry. "What happened then?"

He began to stroke her hair again, almost as if he didn't realize he was doing it. She sighed, waiting, soaking in the gentleness of this big, strong man.

"I'd imagined the moment for so long, I could hardly believe it had happened the way I planned. But I also knew I could not stay there, could not work with him after that. So I left."

"You . . . left?"

"Aye."

"But where did you go?"

"The Tournament of the North. I'd gone with my father and our overlord many times before. That's where I met Guy three years earlier."

"You had"—she tried to imagine it—"nothing?"

"Nothing," he repeated. "But the hope that I had saved my mother from my father. I begged her to come with me, but she refused. Before I left, I told my father I would be back, and that if he ever touched my mother again, I would kill him."

Her eyes widened. He was serious. "You would have killed your own father?"

"Aye."

Idalia shivered.

"What happened next?" she asked quickly, filling the awkward silence that followed his admission. One she could never hold against him given the circumstances.

"That story, my lady, is for another time. I did manage to secure my position with Lord Bohun at the tournament."

Her heart in her throat, she asked, "Did you ever see your mother again?"

"Only twice after that. Both times I went home, prepared to make good on my promise. But mother insisted he never touched her after that. The third time I found my way back to the home of my birth, she was already dead."

Idalia blinked.

"A fever took her and never left. She died within a fortnight. The other villagers confirmed my father's story."

Idalia cupped his face in her hands.

"You are a good man," she said, meaning every word. "The bravest man I know."

She could tell he did not believe her.

But neither did he dismiss her words. Instead, Lance simply stood there looking at her, his eyes searching for something. Redemption, perhaps?

"There's more." She could sense he'd not told her everything. But Idalia also knew it was all she'd get from him this night.

He ground his jaw, contemplating, but in the end, he did not utter another word.

She wouldn't press him for more. Not yet. Idalia did not have to ask to know he'd told her a story he did not share with many people. Instead of speaking, or releasing the tears that filled her eyes, she stood on her tiptoes and placed her lips on his, attempting to soothe away the pain she saw in his eyes. She'd only wanted to help heal him, but the kiss quickly turned from innocent to something more.

When he claimed her mouth, she answered by pulling him closer.

Which was when she realized her mother was even more prescient than she'd thought.

Idalia was falling in love with the blacksmith.

❧ 16 ❧

"**Y**ou've improved."

Lance sheathed his sword, pleased to hear it. The two of them left the clearing for Lance's private chambers.

"You have not," he said to Guy without smiling, though his friend knew he did not mean it. In fact, Guy Lavallis was an expert swordsman. He'd been raised by mercenaries, knighted by the French king, and was notorious for never losing a match. In every tournament he entered, he came away the victor of the sword, disarming his opponents at will.

It was Guy who'd taught Lance to use a sword upon their first meeting at the Tournament of the North. It was also Guy who'd helped him secure a position with Lord Bohun, one that had ensured he need not return to his father.

Unfortunately, that had also meant leaving behind the one person who'd loved him above all others, the kindest woman who'd ever lived. To this day, Lance was unsure if his mother had told him the truth when she'd claimed his father had stopped the abuse. At the time, he'd taken her at her word.

He'd wanted to believe it.

"For a man in love, your disposition is far from pleasant."

Lance stopped as they returned to his private chambers at the back of the forge.

"I am not a man in love."

Yet his mind went back to the night before, to the countess's confident declaration that her daughter loved him. His friend had been relentless in his interrogation about that meeting, but Lance had refused to tell him anything. Nor would he do so now, out in the open.

As soon as they entered the private chambers behind the forge, Guy unbelted his sword and laid it on the sole table in the place Lance now called home. Though small, it was larger than his last home and not so much bigger than the one in which he was raised.

"Your behavior says otherwise," Guy quibbled.

Lance sat on the bed, hands on his knees.

"You're certain there is no mission to which you should be attending?"

Guy's impertinent smile was his answer.

"Since securing Stanton's support is essential, no. After last eve, I've a sense I shouldn't leave the job solely to you."

He shouldn't ask questions to which he already knew the answer.

Both men fell silent.

For a man in love.

He had never been in love before. He'd bedded women, but only those with little expectation of a future with him. Widows, mostly.

Idalia was different.

He mourned every moment they were not together even though he knew he should be concentrating on the task at hand. And while he'd heard some encouraging news today—the earl had apparently paid a visit the previous month to a border lord who was vocal with his disdain for the king's current practices—Lance's thoughts were filled with Idalia.

And her mother. Would she truly welcome a blacksmith as her daughter's husband? It seemed unlikely, despite her words.

"You are distracted."

Lance did not deny it.

"While we sit here at Stanton, the king continues to wreak havoc on all of our lives. Even Stanton's own village shows signs of peasants' suffering courtesy of John's outrageous taxes."

Also true.

"Lance? For Christ's sake, are you listening to me?"

Accustomed to his friend's fiery temper, he ignored the tone and answered his question. "Aye. And am getting closer to the truth. When the time is right, I will ask for an audience."

"Ask *her*." Guy began pacing his small room. "A few poignant questions and you'll have the information you need. Don't be a fool, Lance."

He was afraid it may be too late for that.

"Listen to me." Guy stopped directly in front of him. "How do you think this ends?"

Lance clenched his hands into fists at his sides.

"Stanton will support our order," Guy continued, "or he will not. Either way, we'll end up leaving. As comfortable as this may be"—he swept his hands around to indicate the chambers—"it is not your home."

Though Guy's words rang true, Lance disliked hearing them aloud.

"An earl's daughter deserves more than a blacksmith for a husband," he said, his voice flat.

Guy's lips tightened. "I said no such thing."

"You did not need to."

Of course, it was true. If her mother's suggestion had made him imagine, only for a moment, waking up beside Idalia, blessedly naked and sated, it was his own stubborn fault.

"If you were a king, it would not matter."

Lance looked up.

"If there is any man less willing to accept a chance at happiness than you, I don't know of him. Not that I am suggesting your happiness should be found with this particular woman."

He was becoming more and more impatient with this conversation. "My happiness does not matter. Nor does yours. What matters," he said firmly, thinking of Lord Bohun's inability to properly feed his people "is the Order of the Broken Blade."

"If you truly believe that"—Guy's expression softened—"then talk to her."

Talk to Idalia about her father.

Such a simple request. But if Lance questioned her about her father's loyalties, he knew it would forever mar their time together.

I could tell her everything.

Lance dismissed the thought as soon as it came to him. His duty was to the order and his country. Not a woman he'd just met, no matter how lovely, or kind.

He wasn't coming.

Idalia waited at their usual spot, one which had been hers alone for so many years. And she'd been content with that. Until now.

When a crack of thunder sounded in the distance, Idalia took it as a sign it was time to leave. Either that or get her mother's favorite gown wet as the rain looked to soon be coming. Lifting the violet material, she concentrated on memories of her mother instead of . . . him.

This gown had come as a surprise. A gift for May Day. She remembered the day her mother had given it to her—she'd burst into Idalia's room. Roysa and Marina had both been with her, Roysa in a beautiful yellow gown. Marina had carried this violet confection in her arms.

Idalia had sensed her mother was eager to please her, so she'd exclaimed over the vibrant color of the new gown while listening to her sister's exclamations of delight.

What a lovely day that had been. It seemed so long ago now.

When the rain came more quickly than she'd expected, Idalia ran to the hall. She made it through the doors, which the servants opened for her just before the rain turned into a deluge. The heavy doors were closed behind her, and Idalia nodded her thanks— only to reel backward when she saw her father turn the corner directly in front of her.

"Father," she exclaimed.

"Ah, there you are."

Dawson came running up from behind him. Apparently he'd been looking for her as well. Idalia's heart sank. "Is it Mother?"

The two exchanged an inscrutable look, frowning.

"Of sorts," her father said. And before he could utter another word, Idalia took off in the direction of her chamber.

"Hold, daughter," he called behind her. "Your mother is well."

She stopped.

"Well? But . . ."

"She bade me seek you out."

No words could have alarmed her more. Had she

told him about Lance after all? Her father would not, she was certain, share her mother's sentiments.

Did it matter? If he didn't come tonight, surely it was because he'd been repelled by her mother's words.

Her father nodded to Dawson, who left them. The hall was far from empty as servants moved the trestle tables to the sides of the room to prepare for the night. Ushering her to a private alcove, her father indicated that she should sit.

"What did she"—Idalia swallowed—"tell you?"

"That she told you of her first marriage," he said, without preamble.

Oh.

Idalia resisted asking if her mother had said anything else, but since he did not seem to be flying into a rage, she guessed he didn't know all.

"I was surprised," she hedged, unsure of what else to say.

"That's to be expected."

Idalia waited.

"She also warned me."

Her heart pounded uncomfortably in her chest.

"Warned you?"

Her father's eyes had always fascinated her. Their shade was somewhere between brown and green and blue. If she were to ask three people the color, they would each give a different answer.

She watched them narrow.

"You are not the lady of Stanton."

Idalia's breath caught. Did he think she'd been acting above her station in the castle?

"I mean to say, with Roysa gone and your mother —" he frowned—"ill, we have . . . *I* have relied on you, perhaps more so than I should."

Idalia let out a breath, grateful to have misunderstood. "I do not mind, Father," she said truthfully.

"Stanton Castle is my home, and it brings me great joy to care for it. To care for its people."

When he didn't respond, Idalia wondered if she'd said something wrong.

"It is my duty to protect you, your mother and sister, and all of Stanton."

"Of course. I did not mean—"

"I fear I am not making myself clear."

She hated to agree with him on that point, but she didn't quite understand what he meant to say.

"There is nothing more important to me," he said, as if that clarified his words.

Unfortunately, it did not.

"I don't understand."

"There are things . . . things we cannot control, happening in our country right now."

Oh. He spoke of the king.

Although he'd never outright said so, she knew her father disagreed with many of King John's policies. She waited patiently, expecting him to say more, but he did not. Perhaps she should feel grateful for what little he had revealed. This was as much as her father ever spoke to her of anything other than matters of the household.

"I understand, Father."

And she thought she did. Though he was reticent on the matter, others talked openly about what was happening in their country. About the taxes and war with France. One that none wanted except for their king.

"Very good," he said, visibly more relaxed than he'd been before. "Then I'll leave you to"—he looked around the hall—"the evening," he finished. "Or what is left of it."

She stood when he did.

"Thank you, Father."

Though he did not smile, exactly, the corners of

his mouth lifted ever so slightly. But his eyes were troubled. Because of Mother? The situation with the king?

There was one person who would know what vexed her father, and though the hour was late, she thought a visit with Mother might just take her mind off Lance.

Even though her mother was the one who had, however unintentionally, scared him off.

Just as well. What Idalia planned to tell him this eve would have likely done so as effectively as her mother's words.

If not more so.

❧ 17 ❧

He was a coward.

For two days, Lance avoided the hall. Avoided the Small Tower.

Avoided her.

Again.

Though he'd made more progress in his secret campaign to ally Stanton to their cause, befriending a sergeant who was free with his opinions of the king, Lance continued to disappoint everyone around him.

Guy could not understand why he'd not used his connection with Idalia to his advantage. Idalia likely hated him for thinking he'd abandoned her the moment her mother spoke of commitment.

Being with Idalia did not scare him. What scared him was the fact that he was dreaming of a future with the earl's daughter—a future that could never come to pass.

Such thoughts would be ruinous for him personally, and also for their mission.

And so, he'd taken the coward's way out and avoided her. Unfortunately, he could not avoid Guy, who slammed the door to the forge so hard Lance would likely have to remake its hinges.

"The boys are gone?"

Lance looked around the empty shop, already beginning to fill with shadows now that the door was closed. "Nay, both Miles and Daryon are hiding beneath the bench."

When Guy didn't smile, Lance knew something was wrong. Unlike him, the mercenary was usually as quick with his grins as he was with his gibes.

"What is it?"

"John has secured Bande de Valeur."

It could not be. Bande de Valeur was one of the oldest and most powerful French mercenary armies in existence. In securing their protection, the king exposed his mistrust of his own army. This was as close to an admission of dissent as he'd ever been willing to display.

Lance sank onto the bench. "Who told you this?"

"A merchant passing through brought the news. You'll find all of Stanton talking about it."

"None would know of our order," he thought aloud, "but neither have we heard of any other true resistance forming."

While many of the barons, especially the Northern lords, were unhappy with John's increasingly erratic policies, nothing more than whispers had been heard against him thus far.

"If this is true . . ."

The king was even more foolish than they'd thought. It was an open provocation against his own people. But it was a problem too—

"If it is true, the Order of the Blade will meet with more resistance than we imagined," Lance finished.

The Bande de Valeur was large, its men notoriously ruthless.

Guy was in a position to know.

He'd fought with them once.

"I will turn them around," Guy said, his hands

fisting at his sides. "Aceline de Chabannes is a bastard, but he is an intelligent one. With enough persuasion, he can be brought around to our way of thinking."

"And how do you intend to persuade him? With the truth?"

"Perhaps. And coin, of course. I will speak with Conrad and Terric first."

"Wealthy men, both. But neither have the amount of coin it will take to match the king's coffers."

A fact that did not seem to discourage his friend.

He shook his head emphatically. "They cannot fight for John. We cannot allow it to happen."

Lance agreed—the routiers' presence in England would be a major setback. But he did not see how Guy could possibly hope to persuade an entire company, promised riches from the English king, to turn back to France.

Still, if anyone could do it, Guy could.

"Then go." He stood, extending his arm. Guy took it in his own, clasping his hand around Lance's forearm in a parting gesture as old as their friendship.

"I will gain Stanton's support if he is so inclined to give it."

Guy nodded once, resolutely. "I know you will. Until we meet again, my friend."

Despite knowing of the complications Lance had created for himself, Guy had faith in him. That knowledge bolstered him to do what needed to be done.

"Until we meet again," he repeated.

With a nod, Guy was gone. Which meant Lance had little time for self-indulgence. He could no longer entertain his feelings for Idalia. He had come here for a reason.

And the time to execute his mission was now.

IDALIA AND HER SISTER RODE SIDE BY SIDE AWAY from the castle.

When Tilly was younger, she'd never left Idalia's side. Now Idalia wished she'd not complained about having an ever-present shadow. Those sweet moments had become rarer and rarer as her sister grew into a young woman.

It was market day—always a lively affair—and Idalia had never been more grateful for the distraction. The market in Stanton's village was distinguished by the covered stalls her father had commissioned for the vendors. These were especially attractive to cloth sellers who often wrestled with the elements, as did other merchants.

"A fine day for market," Tilly said, as if she could hear Idalia's thoughts.

"Aye. I was just thinking of the improvements Father made over the years."

"And no doubt you have ideas on how to further improve upon them."

Idalia smiled despite her heavy heart. If Tilly noticed she was not quite herself, her sister did not comment on it. Instead, they spoke of the market and speculated about Roysa's well-being. Her letters came less often, and she'd not been back home to visit yet.

Two things they did not discuss.

Mother. Or the blacksmith.

Not that Tilly knew anything about her relationship with Lance. Of course, "relationship" was the wrong word for it. He'd not sought her out since missing their last meeting.

If her mother's speech scared him from her so easily, then he was not the man for her.

Or so she'd been telling herself these past few days.

"No garlic today," she said, breaking their unspoken agreement not to speak of Mother's condition.

"The new physician should have been here by now," her sister said. Indeed. Idalia reminded herself to speak about it with Father when they returned.

Rounding a bend in the road, they could hear the market square even though they could not yet see it. Voices rose up above the treetops. The clanging metal reminded her of the forge.

Nay. I will not think of him.

An impossible feat given the very man she was supposed to forget called out her name from behind her as she and Tilly arrived at the market.

"My lady."

He rode up alongside her, which was apparently Tilly's cue to leave. If Idalia hadn't known better, she would have suspected the little minx had planned it. Spurring her mount forward, Idalia called back a quick farewell.

Although Idalia wasn't actually alone with Lance, given the throngs of people all around him, she very keenly felt his presence.

"Master Lance."

She continued in her approach toward the stables, refusing to look at him. While he fell in line with her, Lance did not speak until they'd dismounted and handed over their mounts.

"I'm surprised to see you here," she said at last.

The smith worked as hard, if not harder, than their previous smith. A fact many seemed to have noticed. Of late she'd heard his name on the lips of more than one man and woman about Stanton, and while she was glad of it for his sake, she found it difficult to listen to talk of him.

It reminded her of that day.

Of what he did to her, and the way her body had responded to him.

Pretending she did not care seemed to work much better without him standing by her side.

"I've heard much about market day and was curious."

He walked with her past stalls of fresh fruit and cloth. Idalia should have stopped by now—she had quite a bit of shopping to do for Cook and Dawson—but neither her feet nor mouth seemed to be functioning well at the moment.

"Stanton has one of only three market charters in all of Northumbria," she said without thinking.

"And has utilized it well. Covered stalls?"

"My father's idea. He hoped it would attract unique vendors, which would encourage people from other villages to travel here for market day."

She nodded and smiled to each of the vendors they passed, pretending not to notice curious looks Lance was receiving. Idalia made her way to a table filled with cheeses of all kinds, but to her surprise, Lance stayed at her side. After a quick negotiation and agreement to have her purchase sent to Stanton's kitchens, they continued on their way.

"You did that well." Lance was looking back at the merchant. "I don't think I could have gotten his price so low."

"Being the earl's daughter has its advantages."

There was much she wanted to say, but none of it would be proper, especially not here, where anyone might hear them. Instead, Idalia pretended it was perfectly normal to have kissed her, on more than one occasion.

And then there was the small matter of the night he'd lifted her skirts with his hand and brought her the most unimaginable pleasure with his fingers inside her.

God's teeth. Idalia, stop!

"There is a market town in France known for its

exquisite cloth. The lord there built a structure," he pointed to one of the stalls, "like this one, but much larger. More than ten merchants fit inside."

"Ten?"

"Aye. It stands in the square's center, and neither snow nor rain can disturb the merchants and those who deal with them."

Idalia stopped, attempting to imagine such a thing.

"You've seen this?"

Lance stopped with her, and by God, he licked his lips. Nay, just the top lip. And just enough for her to see his tongue and be reminded of what it felt like on hers. She remembered the first time she'd seen him do that.

I am hopeless.

"I have."

They stood in the middle of the road. Idalia knew she should move on, without him, but she had difficulty looking away.

"You could explain it to my father?"

He hesitated.

It was a simple question, but Lance did not answer for some time.

"Aye," he said finally. "I could."

"Good."

When she began to walk again, he reached out to stop her. Then, likely realizing they stood in the middle of a crowded market, he pulled his hand back as if burned.

"Apologies, my lady."

Idalia lowered her voice. "For touching me just now?" She lifted her chin. "Or for something else?"

"For all of it. And more."

Idalia had no idea what he meant. She only knew she must get away from him. Lance made it difficult for her to use the wits she knew she possessed.

She took a step away from him, but he stopped her with his words this time.

"Will you meet me tonight?"

She froze.

Nay. The answer is nay.

Instead, she turned and found herself asking, "Will you show up this time?"

Though he looked apologetic, he did not utter any words of apology. Instead, he nodded.

"I will."

Still, she planned to walk away. She might have done it too, if not for what he said next.

"Please?"

She should say no. Idalia knew enough to guard her heart against a man her father would never accept. One who clearly wanted nothing more than stolen moments of passion.

And yet, this man had a way of making her forget all that she *should* do.

"Aye. I will meet you."

This time, he let her leave.

Fool.

Idalia wasn't sure if she referred to the blacksmith . . . or herself.

❧ 18 ❧

Lance cursed himself as he climbed the stairs to the top of the Small Tower. He should be avoiding Idalia, for her sake. He knew he'd been right to encourage an invitation to talk to the earl about the market stalls. It would provide him the opportunity he needed to confirm Stanton's position on the king.

No doubt, Stanton was unhappy with the king. At least, his men were unhappy with him. Which was likely a reflection of their lord's views. But he hated to embroil Idalia in his machinations. She was unaware of his real motives and nothing good could come of meeting her in secret. He knew only that he'd hurt her and wanted an opportunity to explain. Not that he could give her a full explanation, of course, but she deserved something.

And yet, while he hadn't asked to see her for the sake of the order, Lance knew it was time for him to ask a few pointed questions of the lady of Stanton.

He owed it to the order.

So why did all thoughts of them flee his mind the moment he opened that door?

She was as lovely as she'd been earlier, walking beside him at the market. But even though she wore the same gown, her hair still falling around her shoulders, somehow Lady Idalia appeared more regal now. Chin held high, she was every bit the earl's daughter, a competent young woman who cared for everyone around her.

His mother would have adored her. Though she seemed to have little notion of her own value, Idalia was absolutely perfect in every other way.

"You have no compare," he blurted out. Not the words he'd meant to say, but they were true nonetheless—and she needed to hear them.

"You must not have met many ladies in your time."

"Why do you say such things?"

She walked toward him as warily as he'd expect after what he had done.

"If you knew my sister—"

"A lovely woman, I am sure. But still, I say it again, you have no compare." He put as much meaning into the words as he could, but she still did not appear convinced.

"And yet, you failed to come, failed to meet me."

"That had nothing to do with you."

The bitter laugh that escaped her lips was not Idalia. He hated that he was the cause of her pain.

"Listen to me." He took her hands despite his vow not to touch her. Looking into her eyes, he implored her to understand. "Nothing would please me more than to make you mine."

And it was true.

"But I am simply a smith."

"A master smith."

"But a blacksmith nonetheless. Your mother may have . . . unique views on the matter. But your father would not agree with them, I am sure of it."

Idalia did not argue that point.

"I didn't come to you that night because"—he swallowed—"I was scared."

"I would not imagine a man like you to be afraid of anything."

Lance was immediately brought back to his childhood home, where he'd lain in bed pretending to sleep. Listening for the telltale shouts that signaled his father had drunk too much ale.

"I have been afraid of plenty."

Lance circled her palms with his thumbs, willing her to believe his actions were not a reflection on her. Willing her to see herself as he saw her. As perfect.

He knew he shouldn't tell her how he felt. It wouldn't do anything other than frustrate both of them, and yet the words flowed from his lips. "Most especially I'm afraid to have fallen in love with a woman who cannot be mine."

"What did you say?"

"It does not matter. This . . . this cannot be."

Her lips parted in surprise more than desire, but Lance's body reacted nonetheless.

"Lance—"

"This cannot be," he repeated, as much to himself as to her. But Idalia did not appear to be listening any longer. She closed the distance between them, and he prayed for strength.

"Kiss me," she said, tipping her head up to him.

"Idalia, there's much you do not understand."

"Kiss me."

He wanted to do that and so much more.

Although he knew he couldn't have her, maybe he could at least have this. One kiss.

Their mouths melded together as if they were designed for it. As if he'd been molded for this one person whose sweet scent filled his soul with a greater longing than anything he'd felt in his life—and she for him.

Lance froze when her hand moved from his shoulder down the front of his chest, and lower. She did not stop. Lower still until . . .

He tore his mouth from hers.

"Nay, Idalia."

She pulled her hand away, misunderstanding.

"Please understand. There's nothing I would love more . . ."

"I just . . . you gave me such pleasure. I thought . . ." Her shoulders sagged. "I thought perhaps I could do the same."

His jaw dropped.

"You. Cannot." He forced himself to swallow. "I would welcome it more than you know, but—"

When she realized why he'd stopped her, her hand began to move once more.

Lance had always considered himself a strong man. Or at least he had since the day he'd hit his father. Now he knew otherwise.

He was as weak as a newborn babe.

When her hand rested fully on top of him, he swore an oath in answer to her silent question. She didn't know how to proceed. And he should not be the one to show her.

But damned if he didn't untie the strings that would give her access, guiding her hand and wrapping it around his hardened cock.

As she stroked him, following his hand as a guide, Idalia looked into his eyes and smiled. This was the smile of a woman who'd just learned she wielded a secret power. For if she asked for the world right now, Lance would give it gladly.

"'Tis both smooth and hard."

He removed his hand from hers and gripped her shoulders.

"I never imagined . . ."

"Idalia." He tossed his head back and closed his eyes.

"Does it feel as good as your fingers did inside me?"

She had no idea.

He had to stop her now. Grabbing her hand, he spun her around and pinned her to the wall behind them. Knowing they were hidden from view, he took her mouth in a passionate kiss, claiming her in the only way he could.

Even though he pressed against her, Lance knew she must feel very little through the layers of her gown, but he didn't dare lift it. The urge to be inside her was too great. He could make her come again, but it seemed an empty gesture. She deserved more than a quick release.

She deserved everything.

"I would be inside you," he whispered in her ear before nipping it with his teeth. "I would bury myself so deep, we would be as one."

He kissed behind her ear, emboldened by each exhale, her heavy breathing matching his own.

"I would make love to you, sweet Idalia, and show you what a valuable treasure you are."

She gripped the fabric of his shirt.

"If you were mine, I would love you with my mouth," he continued.

He pulled back, realizing she didn't understand. Perversely, he wanted her to. Wanted her to spend each night imagining all the things they might do to each other if they were free to do as they wished. It was how he'd spent his nights since coming to Stanton.

"Aye, I would taste you there." He glanced down to the apex of her legs, his meaning unmistakable this time.

"Surely not."

She was surprised, but intrigued. If only he could show her.

What in God's teeth are you doing? She's not for the likes of you, you fool.

"I shouldn't have said such a thing."

"Why?" She stepped back, and Lance had never been so grateful. Near her, he could not think. Could not reason. When he was with Idalia, the world fell away.

"You know why. I am a smith. You are an earl's daughter."

"Whose mother condoned . . . whatever this is. Tell me, Lance. What is this, between us?"

If only he knew. He only understood he couldn't stay away from her.

"Your words earlier, they mean nothing?"

"Your father—"

"Does not know you. Not as I do."

"You know little of me," he said, thinking of the order. The secrets he held might change her mind about him. They might make her regret what she'd said and shared. He thought again of his friends, and of everything they stood to lose should the Earl of Stanton refuse to support their cause.

He needed to speak with the man, to know his mind.

"I know you've been hurt," she said, her eyes shining. "I know you treat your apprentices as if they were your sons. Their mother can speak of little else but you. And I know when I'm with you, I feel . . ."

"Stop."

He'd asked her to stop, but when she did, Lance desperately wanted to know what she'd intended to say. He nearly asked her to finish.

But duty bound him, and so he did what he must.

"Introduce me to your father."

She misunderstood, of course. Took it as a sign of

encouragement for them, when it was just the opposite.

The smile she gave Lance made him feel as if he'd fallen into the forge's fire. His chest burned with the truth. Not for the first time, he thought to tell her all. Perhaps she would understand? Perhaps her father might even surprise them both with his acceptance of the match?

Aye, a smith and a traitor to the king.

The man would likely have him tossed in the dungeon before he would accept him as a suitor for his daughter.

And if he supports our cause?

There was a better chance of that than the earl supporting a claim to his daughter. And now he'd given her false hope.

Was there a worse man alive than he?

❧ 19 ❧

"He is glorious."

Although Idalia had meant to keep her entanglement with Lance to herself for the time being, her resolution hadn't lasted long. Love loosened a person's tongue, it turned out, for she'd already told her maid everything.

"I love him," she confessed, then hastened to add, "I know, 'tis a silly thing to say about a man I met mere weeks ago, but Leana, if you could only speak at length to him. Well," she considered, "that may not convince you right away. He actually appears quite dour at times."

"You do remember I've already met him." Leana finished tying the laces on her side.

Idalia lowered her arm and smoothed out her surcoat.

"But you did not get to know him."

"I'm happy for you, Idalia, truly, but are you certain"—Leana cleared her throat—"your father will approve?"

"I am."

She avoided Leana's gaze. It was a lie and both women knew it. Still, Lance had asked for a meeting —and she'd arranged it with her father.

"I spoke to Mother this morn. She asked that I bring Lance to her for an extended visit."

"How does she fare today?"

"The same," she admitted. "I tried to convince her to walk about the chamber, but her stomach pained her too much."

Her mother thought she was dying, that she would never get well, but Idalia refused to accept it as a possibility. The physician from London was due to arrive any day.

Her mother would get well. She simply must.

"Are you ready?"

She looked down at her pale yellow kirtle, topped with a royal blue surcoat.

Stanton colors.

Her father adored them and never failed to comment when she, or her sisters, wore them. Unlike Roysa and Tilly, Idalia rarely attempted to curry approval, but today, she could use every bit of help she could get.

Leana was certainly right: convincing her father she should marry for love would not be a simple matter. Even the countess, who'd suggested the match, agreed with her on that.

But Idalia was determined. A trait she had, according to her mother, inherited directly from the very man she sought to convince.

First, however, she needed to find Lance. They'd agreed to meet just inside the hall so she could properly present him to her father. Sure enough, that was exactly where she found him, standing just inside the entranceway. Others always appeared so small standing next to the two massive oak doors. But not he. Not Lance.

He was speaking to Dawson when she approached.

"Good day," she called to them both.

Thankfully, Dawson did not seem to notice the lingering, appreciative look Lance gave her as she came near.

"Good day, my lady," Dawson said. "If you'll pardon me, I believe there are visitors I must attend to."

Idalia had not heard of any visitors but was glad Dawson was assuming the role she normally would have taken voluntarily. She inclined her head toward the back of the hall. Her father waited in the solar chamber adjacent to where she and Lance now stood. Under normal circumstances, no one bothered him in there.

"Good day, Lady Idalia."

She couldn't discern his expression. Although his expression was often serious, it looked . . . wary . . . and something else.

"You're worried?" she asked.

When she'd found Lance earlier in the forge to advise him of the meeting, he'd not said much at all. They'd agreed this would be a formal welcome to Stanton, nothing more. She'd assured him it was not so unusual that such a meeting should occur.

And then? Idalia was not sure. She'd wished to ask Lance as much, but in the back of her mind she'd heard her sisters accusing her of overplanning. Her strengths, they often said, were also her faults, and Idalia tended to agree. For once, she'd decided to leave the arrangements to someone else.

Her father was waiting at the door when they reached the solar.

"Do come inside and sit."

Lance bowed, which made her internally wince— she'd forgotten to warn him that her father disliked formality—and they all took a seat, Lance and Idalia across from her father. A large oak desk, one hand-crafted for her grandfather, separated them.

"My daughter speaks highly of you, Master Lance."

Lance seemed surprised by her father's use of his name. But her father never forgot a name. Ever.

"As she does of you, my lord."

"I would welcome you to Stanton, once again. I do hope the task of replacing Master Roland has not proven too difficult?"

"It has not, my lord. I find the people here quite welcoming. Your daughter included."

He said it so smoothly Idalia nearly laughed aloud. Welcoming, indeed.

"And how do you find the forge?"

"Well appointed and in need of little."

If Lance had not conversed with nobility often, as he claimed, it was difficult to discern. Her father would appreciate his firm, unwavering tone. And if her father's smile were any indication, he was already impressed.

Sitting back in his seat, he continued to scrutinize Lance without even glancing her way. Which was typical, though the dismissal stung no less because of its frequency.

"Well," he said at last, "if you are in need of anything, you've only to ask Dawson."

Idalia looked down to her hands, which she'd folded in her lap.

"Or Lady Idalia, I presume," Lance replied, "as she seems to have a firm handle on castle affairs."

Her head shot up. Would her father take it as a rebuke? It did not seem so, but she would have to warn Lance in the future not to praise her in such a way. She did not want her father to think Lance's words were a slight to the seneschal whom he so adored.

"As such," her father responded.

"If I may ask a question, my lord?"

Idalia held her breath. Even if her father approved of Lance, it was near certain he wouldn't approve of Lance for her. Add in a bad first impression, and her mother's well wishes would mean little.

"Certainly."

"My previous lord required that I incorporate one of the crown's three lions on all armor, and I wondered if my lord asks the same of me?"

What in the heavens?

It was the kind of question she could have answered in a trice. Although she'd heard of such a practice before, Roland had certainly never been required to do such a thing. Why hadn't Lance asked her or even Dawson?

And why was her father looking at Lance so seriously, as if he were contemplating his answer, which would most certainly be no.

"Did such a request aggrieve you?" her father finally asked.

Lance answered immediately. "It did, my lord. If I may be so bold as to admit such a thing."

The tone of the meeting had changed. And although she was astute enough to understand as much, Idalia had no idea what had happened. She did, however, plan to find out.

"Then you will be pleased to know I would not require it of you or any smith of Stanton."

For the first time that afternoon, Lance seemed to relax.

Idalia barely listened to the pleasantries that passed between the men until her father finally remembered she was present.

"I will see to your mother this eve."

It was her custom to do so, but she'd not argue with her father. Especially in front of a guest.

"Very well," she said, bowing her head. And then remembered the stalls.

"Father, Master Lance told me of an idea for the market. Something he's seen before in France that may be of interest."

Lance explained what he had seen, encouraging her into the conversation. Her father seemed pleased by the idea and promised to give it further thought.

"If that is all?" Her father dismissed them both.

Lance understood and stood, Idalia doing the same as they made their way out of the solar.

"Ahh, my lady." Dawson swooped down on them the moment they stepped into the hall, like a bird that had been lying in wait for its prey. "We have visitors. If you would assist me in welcoming them?"

She looked at Lance, who didn't meet her eye. Something had been odd about that meeting, and she would discover what it was. But not, it seemed, at this moment.

"Of course. If you will pardon me, Master Lance?"

Did Lance appear relieved as he nodded in parting? He had defended her in there, and yet, she could not shake the feeling that he had misled her as well.

They were set to meet again at the Small Tower that evening, but Idalia was not patient enough to wait so long. She would see to the visitors and then visit the forge.

She had a question or two for Lance.

༄ 20 ༅

When Lance opened the door of his private
chambers, he didn't expect to see Miles
on the other side. He'd sent the boys
home for the day not long ago and had just returned
from a cold wash in the river.

"Good eve, Master Lance."

Miles stuck out his arms, handing him what
looked like a loaf of bread covered in a white cloth.

"Gyngerbrede," he confirmed. "My ma made it
herself. She says it's to thank you for bein' so kind
to us."

"Many thanks to her, Miles." The sweet scent
reached him as he took the bread. It was one of his
mother's favorites, a fact he'd relayed to the boys just
the day before.

When Daryon had asked about his parents.

As usual, he'd spoken only of his mother. Idalia
was one of the only people he'd told about his father.
Other than her, only the rest of the other members of
the order knew the truth.

"Master Lance?"

The boy looked up at him with a reverence he
didn't deserve. It struck him that it would be hard to

leave Stanton—and not just because of the beautiful, stately woman who had his heart.

"Aye?"

"Will you show us how to use the cross-pein hammer to draw out iron? My da says you could likely do anything, even that."

An easy enough request. "Aye, we will do it on the morrow. Now run along before you miss supper," he said. Miles had already turned and started running. "And give thanks to your mother for the bread."

Miles reached his hand up and waved.

A good lad. Both of them were. And their mother had shown him a kindness he didn't deserve.

Guilt pressed into him, his constant companion of late. He hadn't been honest with these people, yet they'd invited him in and made him feel a sense of belonging he had not experienced with anyone other than the other men in the order.

Lance was about to close the door when he saw her.

Dressed all in white, she looked like an avenging angel, gliding down the hill to smite him.

"White," he said as she circled around the forge, "is not the most practical color to wear here."

Idalia stopped before him. Her hair was unbound, falling in waves down her back, and he longed to reach out and touch it. He held his hands together to stop himself.

"A kitchen maid spilled sauce verte on the other."

But Idalia had not come to him to speak of spilled sauces.

"I'm surprised you're not overseeing supper?"

"I'm surprised you did not mention your concern over the engraving to me."

And there it was.

Though the question had revealed the earl's leanings, giving him exactly the information he needed, it had come at a price.

"I apologize for making you uncomfortable."

She waited, but Lance would say no more. Anything else he uttered would be a lie, and he'd lied to her already. As it had been many times before, the truth lay on his tongue, its utterance so close to fruition. But he could not do it. Lance had little to offer the order. No coin or armies of men. Nothing but his loyalty and the success of this mission.

"Would you come in?" he said finally. "I've little to offer but"—he lifted his hand—"bread and ale, though I would very much welcome your company."

She would refuse. Which was for the best, really. If anyone saw her enter his chambers, it would be bad for both of them.

"I do not understand you."

Most didn't.

"Do you need to go to the hall?" he pressed.

Idalia shook her head. "Dawson has been left in charge. My father is seeing to my mother and Tilly is supping in her chamber. A new kitten found its way to the keep, and she worried it would be trounced upon in the hall. She refuses to leave him."

She shrugged, as if to say "sisters." But Lance was an only child. The closest he had to a sibling was Guy. And the others in the order.

He stepped back, willing her to follow. Knowing she should not. It was foolish of him to ask—and reckless, besides.

"I beg you, come inside. I will not touch you. That is a promise."

She looked at him curiously then. "You believe that is what I want? For you to stay away from me?"

He took another step back.

Idalia followed.

"When we are together, it can be difficult to"—he

took in a deep breath as she walked past him —"converse."

God forgive him if he didn't nearly reach for her despite his words. He kept thinking of her hand on him, stroking. Her breasts hugged by the white material.

"Is that a common affliction when two people . . ." She trailed off, looking up at him with side eyes.

"When two people . . . ?" he prompted.

"You vow not to touch me, but look at me so."

He inclined his hand, gesturing for her to sit at a small table inside. Though the room was sparsely furnished, Roland had decorated it with iron embellishments that gave it a unique quality Lance rather liked. Already it felt like home.

Again, it struck him that it would be difficult to leave this place.

He placed the bread between them and poured two mugs of ale. He sat opposite her, thinking how odd it was she fit so well at the head table in a hall fit for a king but also here, at this modest smith's table, with him. He truly knew no other lady like her.

Already, he knew he'd never meet her equal.

"What were your intentions for the meeting with my father?"

Lance nearly spat out the ale he'd just swallowed. Somehow, he managed to hold it down.

"To make his acquaintance, as we discussed."

"For what purpose?"

It was a fair question, of course, and one he'd expected. So why had he invited her inside?

He couldn't help himself around Idalia. Being with her stole his reason and common sense. It put his feelings in the forefront, something unusual for him.

Not ready to answer her truthfully, and unwilling to lie to her, he instead tried to explain his dilemma. "When my mother died," he said softly, "I blamed myself for not being there, but it was also her wish for me to leave." He took a swig of ale. "It was the most difficult decision I'd ever made. If I had stayed, I would have killed him eventually."

It was not easy to admit, but Lance firmly believed it to be true.

"Worse," he added, "I'd have felt no remorse."

"You would have."

He shook his head. "One time, he tossed her onto the ground and put his foot to her throat. I'd come to the door, intending to stop him. Instead, I stood there, hands shaking, watching as she tried unsuccessfully to speak. When I finally took a step toward them, my father stopped me with one glance."

Another swig.

"I hated him for the way he treated my mother, but I also hated that he rendered me powerless. Or so I thought at the time."

Lance had not meant to go into such detail, but he found he wanted to open himself to her. To show him the man he was, faults and all. And he wanted to tell her about the order too. He'd wanted that for some time. His vow had stopped him—as had the realization that doing so would endanger not just him and his mission but also Guy, Terric, and Conrad. And yet . . . perhaps there was a way to gauge her receptiveness.

"Tell me a story," he said, looking into her eyes. "I asked your father about the king's inscription. What do you think of it. Of him?"

"Of the king?" she asked, surprise in her gaze.

"Aye."

Lance opened the cloth and nodded to the freshly baked bread. He tore off a piece, and Idalia did the same.

"I know little of him, though I've heard stories of his father, of course."

"Whom your own father served?"

"Aye. But I know little of Prince John . . ." She took a bite of the bread. "Other than that he's our king, of course."

Lance sighed.

"Aye, he is."

Willing her to say more, to give any indication she might be in agreement with their cause, Lance held his breath.

"My father, as you saw, does not allow for me to have an opinion on such matters."

A notion shared by most men in his position. But Lance wanted her to have an opinion. More desperately than he wanted anything in the world.

"But you have one anyway?"

Idalia opened her mouth to speak, and then closed it.

"Nay. I do not."

Which meant he could not risk sharing the order's secrets.

And if she'd said aye? That she hated King John and wished he could be brought to heel? What then? Would you have told her?

Lance was afraid of his answer.

❧ 21 ❧

Lance's hand ran up her leg, ever so slowly.

His touch trailed a path of fire across her skin. Closing her eyes, Idalia concentrated on the roughness of his blacksmith's hand grazing her, even though his touch was soft. Warm. And suddenly, he was *there*.

Urging her thighs to open wider, his fingers then taunted her entrance. Any moment . . . ah, yes. It felt just like that first time, but Idalia wanted more. Much more.

"More," she murmured.

What a glorious, wicked feeling.

"*More.*"

Her eyes flew open. That word hadn't been spoken by her but by her maid, Leana. Nay, she hadn't said "more" but "morn."

"Good morn, my sleepy lady," Leana said softly.

It was dark, certainly not morning yet. She'd been dreaming, fantasizing about what she wished had happened last eve.

"Leana?" she asked into the dark. "Whatever are you about?"

"He's here . . ."

Given the direction of her thoughts, Idalia could

only think of one person that could be about. She sat up so quickly, Leana took a step back from the bed.

"Lance?"

Leana's nose scrunched up, making Idalia realize her mistake. Not Lance. Of course not.

"Who's here?"

It was too early in the morn for riddles.

"The physician."

"The physician? At this time of day?" She swung her legs over the side of the bed at once, fully awake now. "Did he travel all night?"

"Dawson woke me to send for you. He arrived a short time ago. As for traveling through the night, I know nothing of that except . . . he is here already and with your mother."

Idalia didn't even pause long enough to visit the garderobe. She slipped out of her chemise and into the shift and gown Leana had prepared. She chewed on a piece of mint her maid handed her as she tied the laces at her back.

He was here.

Finally.

"Is Father with them?"

"Aye," Leana confirmed. "Shall I wake Tilly as well?"

Idalia started to say nay, then thought better of it. Her sister often accused her of treating her like a child when, in truth, she was closer to womanhood than Idalia would care to admit.

"Aye. Send her to Mother's chamber."

When Leana finished brushing her hair, she gave the maid a quick squeeze of her hand in thanks and bolted from the bedchamber.

Making her way to her mother's chamber, Idalia's heart hammered in her chest, the dream completely forgotten. Or mostly forgotten. She and Lance had talked for hours last eve, the awkwardness between them fading as they shared stories from their youth, and yet he'd held fast to his resolution not to touch her. It was little wonder her waking fantasies had bled into her dreams.

But none of that mattered right now. Nothing mattered except her mother.

If anyone could help her, it was this doctor.

When she entered the chamber, Idalia hastened to her father's side. The physician was standing next to the bed speaking to her mother.

"What's happening?" she whispered.

The man who looked down at her was her father, not the earl. It had taken some time for her to understand that dichotomy. A couple of years earlier, a neighboring baron—and a confidant of the man who was now King John—had visited the hall to ask for Roysa's hand in marriage. Her father had sent Idalia away, saying the matter was a discussion ill-suited for her ears, and she'd run upstairs weeping, seeking her mother's comfort.

Her mother had taught her a lesson Idalia had never forgotten.

The Earl of Stanton was one of the most powerful men in the north. Like his father and grandfather before him, he was continually called upon to balance the king's demands with potential alliances that could alter the course of Stanton's future.

She'd learned two valuable lessons that day.

First, her father was more than just the man who'd sired her. As the Earl of Stanton, he had an obligation to care for his people—and oversee their relationship to their king.

Second, she must never speak ill of either her father or their king to anyone.

Not even the man I love.

Idalia, like her father, despised King John for the

way he treated his people. But neither of them would ever utter such a thing aloud.

To do so would be to court trouble.

"He only just arrived," her father explained, "and has been asking her questions."

Her mother, thank the heavens, was awake. And seemed to be answering the physician's questions with ease. He asked about her headaches and what had been causing them, then inquired about the discoloration of the whites of her eyes.

After a few more questions, the physician turned to them.

"If you will." He looked toward the door.

"I am *not* leaving," Idalia's father said emphatically.

That, the voice of the earl.

She and Marina exchanged a glance, and at Idalia's nod, both of them stepped outside and closed the door. Just as they did, Tilly came bounding around the corner. She'd evidently dressed in a hurry—her slippers were mismatched—and was panting with exertion. If Idalia had to guess, she'd probably raced out the door of her chamber before Leana could correct the mistake.

"What did the doctor say? Is he in there now? Why are you out here?"

"He's said nothing yet," Idalia told her, taking her hand. "I believe he is examining her now. Father refused to leave the chamber."

Marina forced a smile. "I'll be back shortly," she said. "Your mother needs fresh water."

Idalia knew she was likely just as nervous as they were and likely the reason she carried a bowl with her now, as if the task could not wait.

With nothing to do, Tilly began to pace back and forth, and Idalia silently joined her. Every so often they exchanged a glance, but otherwise they did nothing more than pace the corridor. Finally, the door opened.

Idalia ran to the bed where her father sat weeping.

Her father, the Earl of Stanton. He was actually crying, something she'd never seen him do before. Her mother was awake, one hand clasped around her father's while the other rested on his shoulder.

Idalia's chest felt as if it would collapse in on itself. She could not breathe. She could not think. She sunk down onto the other side of the bed, tears welling in her eyes. The sight of her mother, so frail, and her father . . .

This could only mean their worst fears had come to fruition.

She didn't even realize Tilly had sat next to her until she felt the small fingers weave through her own.

"No, no"—her mother placed her hand on Idalia's arm—"I can see you fear the worst, but it is not bad, my sweet. Please, tell them."

Idalia followed her mother's gaze to the physician. The tall, thin man whose eyes had the wizened look of someone who'd witnessed a thousand deaths. And yet, he *smiled* at them.

It was not at all what Idalia had been expecting.

"'Tis a simple matter, really."

Idalia's heart raced.

"She has been consuming large quantities of skullcap for some time, to relieve her headaches. Her body is rejecting the herb."

"What . . . what are you saying?"

The creases around his eyes deepened, as did his smile.

"The skullcap was killing her."

Silence.

"Killing her," Tilly repeated, unable to process the revelation.

"She risks her head pains returning, of course, but I have alternative ways to treat that."

Could it be? She looked at her father more closely. He was composed now, his expression once again inscrutable, but his eyes weren't sad.

Not at all.

Her father had been shedding tears of joy, a fact that caused her own eyes to brim with emotion. She laid her head on her mother's chest, needing to hear the steady beating of her heart. Needing to reassure herself that she was, indeed, okay.

"She should recover fully as the effects of the skullcap abate," she heard the physician say behind her.

Her mother stroked the back of her head. Although Tilly and her father spoke of something, Idalia could focus on nothing beyond the sound of her mother's heart and the feeling of the hand smoothing her hair.

"Will you give us a moment?"

At first, Idalia thought her mother had been speaking to the physician, asking for a moment alone with her family, but when she finally lifted her head, everyone was gone.

"I am so sorry," she said to her mother, for it needed saying. They should have ensured the doctor came much, much sooner.

Her mother wiped away a tear with her thumb. "There is nothing to apologize for, my dear. We are all quite relieved."

"Skullcap," she muttered. "How did we not know?"

Her mother shrugged. "We will not waste time attempting to answer that question. Better to focus on a different one."

"A different question?" As soon as the words left

her mouth, she knew of what her mother spoke. "Lance?"

"Ah, so you no longer refer to him as Master Lance?"

"Mother, we really should be speaking of you. Your health is all I care about."

"Nay, we should not. I'm quite finished with speaking of my health."

Her father wasn't the only member of this family who could quell a discussion with just a few direct words. The countess's ability to be both nurturing and firm in one breath was a feat Idalia only hoped to master in time.

"So?"

There was no denying her mother, especially not now. She told her of Lance's meeting with the earl, the odd question he'd asked, and her visit to his quarters later that eve. She assured her mother they'd done naught but talk and laugh, although she knew perfectly well it had been inappropriate to visit him alone.

"My feelings on the matter have not changed," her mother said. "If you think he is worthy, if you love this man, then I give my blessing."

She heaved a long sigh, for this was something she'd thought of again and again in the past days. "If love is not wanting to be apart from someone for even a moment, wishing you could heal their every pain, and dreaming of being with them every day for the rest of your life, then aye, I love him."

"And he claims to feel the same?"

"He does. But there is something . . . holding him back from me. I know not what."

A knock at the door was followed by her sister's voice. "You cannot have Mama all to yourself, Idalia!"

"She needs to see you." Idalia stood.

"Go to him," her mother said, meeting and holding her gaze. "Tell him how you feel."

"And father?"

Her mother smiled, and though she still looked as ill as she had these past weeks, there was a glint in her eyes that had not been there before.

Her mother would be well, and truly, nothing else mattered.

She swallowed.

Perhaps one thing did.

"I will speak to your father when the time comes. Now go before Tilly breaks down my door."

Wrapping her arms around her mother's frail shoulders, Idalia pushed back the tears that threatened again. No more sadness.

She'd taken care of Stanton in her mother's stead, and now it was her time to take care of herself.

22

Lance swung his hammer, again and again.

As he'd always done when frustrated or angry, he took out his aggression on the metal. But instead of fighting back, it flattened and pulled exactly like it was supposed to.

Daryon pumped the bellows as he reheated the steel and pounded away at it again. It would be some time before the sword took shape, but Lance was grateful for the commission. He'd made enough hinges and nails to last a lifetime.

Forging a sword was a challenge.

Sensing a presence behind him, Lance turned and immediately knew something had happened. Idalia stood at the doorway dressed simply, and somehow lovelier for it. It was impossible not to smile in response to her radiant expression.

"Take over." He held out the steel to Daryon, waiting for him to don his glove. "Finish pounding it, and we'll bevel it when I return."

Daryon took it, looked at his brother, blinked, and then shifted his gaze back to Lance.

"Do you think you can do it?" Lance asked.

"I do."

Miles moved toward the bellows in anticipation.

"Aye, he can do it, and I'll help!" he said, his excitement heartening his brother.

He nodded his approval, leaving his young apprentices to their work as his father's words came back to him.

You may not be ready, but try anyway.

How could such a skilled blacksmith and patient teacher also be such a horrible man?

Shoving the thought aside, he hung his apron near the door and led Idalia outside. She nodded toward his chambers at the back of the forge.

"This cannot be overheard just yet," she explained in a hushed tone.

Once inside, he resisted the urge to take her in his arms. The promise he'd made last eve, not to touch her, had done nothing to alleviate his desire to do so.

In fact, he wondered if it had had the opposite effect.

"My mother," she said the moment he closed the door. "My mother will be well!"

With her hands clasped in front of her, her eyes bright with enthusiasm, Idalia resembled her younger sister more than she did the woman with all the weight of Stanton on her shoulders.

"The physician came early this morn, although I still don't know why he'd arrive at such an odd time. But with all that happened, I never thought to press him on it."

"Tell me," he prodded gently, eager to know the full story.

"He examined Mother, and she will be well! It was the skullcap she took for the pain in her head. The physician said"—she swallowed—"it was killing her."

"The skullcap . . ."

"Aye. The pains in her stomach started soon after she began taking it, although she thought they were related to her headaches. She started to get so sleepy all the time, and then her eyes . . ." She let her words drift off. "Oh, Lance, I am so very happy."

When she threw her arms around his waist, Lance embraced her, pulled her toward him and threaded his hands through her hair. He could feel her heart beating wildly against his chest as a sense of peace washed over him.

He'd feared she would lose her mother, a pain he well understood, but that horror had been averted. Closing his eyes, Lance allowed his relief to settle for a time before he pulled back just slightly.

"No tears," he said, wiping them away with his thumb. "This is a joyous day."

He kissed her without thinking, but the quick touch immediately made him hungry for more. It was as if a fire had been lit as their mouths came together again. It was so natural to deepen the kiss that before long they were both breathless, wanting, needing more.

He was surprised, and grateful, when *she* pulled away. Despite himself, Lance simply could not resist this woman.

"I came here to talk." Idalia tucked a wisp of hair behind her ear.

"About your mother?"

"And . . . us."

That very topic had kept him awake most of the night.

"I need to know." She straightened, and Lance knew it was time to tell her all. He accepted it, and yet he wanted to delay the inevitable just a little. If only because he knew his news would dampen the excitement she felt. "Idalia, you are right. We do need to talk, but I have to get back to the boys. Tonight—"

A rapping at the door interrupted her. Idalia and Lance exchanged a look, and she tucked herself out of view of the door. He waited a moment and then opened it.

Miles stood in the doorway. "Pardon, Master Lance," he said, "but the seneschal came looking for you. Says the earl has agreed to meet you this morn. He returned to the keep . . ." He paused, as if considering his next words, then said, "I saw you walk behind the forge, but I didn't tell him where you were."

Because he'd seen Idalia enter the chambers too.

Lance remained calm despite knowing Idalia had heard everything. He'd asked for another meeting that morn. He felt confident from all he'd learned that the earl would be sympathetic to the order's cause. The time had come to approach him.

"'Tis fine, Miles. Thank you for coming to me."

The boy turned to leave.

"How are the bevels?" he asked.

"Better than yours," the apprentice jested with a grin, walking back to the shop.

Lance would have smiled at the boy's glibness if not for the message he'd brought.

"A meeting with my father?" Idalia asked as soon as he closed the door. She stared at him, waiting for an explanation.

There was no help for it now. She deserved to know everything. Telling her before speaking to the earl was dangerous. Foolish. But Lance owed her this. He could not deny her the truth any longer.

"You planned to speak to him about us?"

"Nay."

Her smile fell—and Lance felt a jolt in his stomach. He hated that he'd stolen her joy, hated, too, that he'd changed things between them.

"I don't understand."

"I plan to ask him to support our order."

Idalia's eyes narrowed.

"A knightly order," he clarified.

"A knightly . . . but, one must be a knight to . . ." Her eyes widened. "Lance?"

"I am a knight. But I'm a blacksmith too," he rushed to add. "One who has seen the people of our country suffer at the hands of a man who cares little for those he rules. A man who brings, even now, French mercenaries to our shores to enforce his will on his people."

"You speak of our king?"

"Aye."

Her back straightened, her expression closed down. "You speak treason."

"I do. But you must understand—"

Her tone was flat, measured. "You came to Stanton to garner my father's support for a rebellion against our king."

"Aye."

She said nothing.

When she moved past him toward the door, he didn't stop her. With one hand on the iron handle, Idalia turned to him, as angry as she'd been joyful when she'd run down to the forge.

Lance hated himself in this moment nearly as much as he had upon learning of his mother's death.

"Did you never think to tell me? To ask *me* of my father's position, of Stanton's position?"

"I tried not to involve you, Idalia. I didn't want to use my relationship with you to further my mission. I never planned to fall in love with you."

Her head dropped, shoulders sagged.

"You are just like him."

With that, she opened the door.

"Like who? Idalia, stay. Please. I would talk about this with you."

When she looked up, Lance was sorry he'd stopped her. He would never forget the look on her face at that moment. Her eyes flat. Lips pinched. So unlike Idalia.

"The man whose approval you seek. Go." She swept her free hand toward the door. "Meet with him. You'll likely find the support you seek, for he despises our king as much as, maybe more than, you do. If you had but asked, I would have told you that long ago."

"Idalia . . ."

She didn't even look at him again. She merely opened the door and walked out.

He thought to stop her, but what could he say? *I'm sorry?* The words seemed hollow even to his own ears.

I love you? If he was right—and judging by Idalia's parting words, he'd been correct in his assessment of the earl's position—could he really risk Lord Stanton's ire by asking for Idalia's hand in marriage?

He, a blacksmith.

At best, Stanton would laugh him out of his hall. At worst, he would refuse to back the order as retaliation for the foolish insult.

You are just like him.

Lance wished he didn't understand her meaning so clearly, but the memory of their first meeting was clear in his mind.

Stanton no doubt loved his daughter, but he certainly did not respect her opinion on anything more important than which dish to serve at supper.

You are just like him.

She was wrong, but it hardly mattered. Idalia hated him.

And he'd earned her hate.

❧ 23 ❦

"**Y**ou came here under the pretense of being a blacksmith."

Well aware that the man seated across from him had the power to throw him in the dungeon, Lance shook his head. "I am a blacksmith. But aye, my purpose here was to secure this meeting."

He'd just told the Earl of Stanton everything, and here he was, thinking of Idalia. Of the hurt he'd caused her.

"Tell me more of this order."

Lance thought back to the horrific occurrence that had banded them into a brotherhood. Conrad's blade. The sickening splash of water. None could have guessed more than ten years later their friendship would have brought them here.

"Guy Lavallis of Cradney Wrens fights as a mercenary."

"And is hailed as the greatest swordsman in England."

"Aye, because it is true."

Lance could not discern the earl's expression, so he continued.

"Terric Kennaugh of Bradon Moor, chief of Clan Kennaugh—"

"And lord of Dromsley here in England."

Lance was not surprised the earl knew of him. Terric's father had acquired Dromsley as a part of his English mother's dowry. It was his by rights, but a counterclaim had been issued by none other than King John's half-brother, the Earl of Salisbury.

"I have no doubt as to why Kennaugh would join a rebellion against the king."

Lance winced. To hear it said aloud by someone outside of the order . . .

"You said there were four?"

He hesitated on the last name, not knowing how the earl would react to learning the son of his old enemy was involved in the enterprise. "The Earl of Licheford."

To his surprise, Stanton did not flinch.

"I'm told the son is more even-tempered than his father?"

"Indeed," he said truthfully. Conrad's father had possessed a legendary temper—one that had caused more conflicts than his fissure with this man.

"What does this order hope to achieve, precisely?"

A fair question.

"To restrain the king's power and force him to negotiate with his barons."

Stanton laughed at that.

"You are a fool to think such a thing is possible."

Inwardly, Lance crumbled under the earl's words. Outwardly, he lifted his chin and pressed on. "We are fools to allow him to continue on his current course unchecked. With the recent loss in France, there's never been a time of more discontent, even among some of the Southern barons. And John knows it. Why do you think he has secured French mercenaries who are even now on their way to England?"

"A bold move, I will admit."

So he would not join them.

Lance began to think ahead. Their path would not be an easy one without Stanton. But they would forge on regardless.

"You have my support."

No four words could have surprised him more.

"You called us fools just a moment ago."

"And you are. I among you. Such a mission is likely doomed, and could very well cost us everything."

Idalia. Her mother, so recently healed. And her sisters . . .

Lance cared little for his own life, but the thought of putting them in danger? Of course, he'd known all along what Stanton's support might meant for Idalia.

But a part of him hadn't believed Stanton would actually join them.

"You are surprised."

"In truth, I am. Your family . . ."

"Will be safe enough if the tide turns. Stanton's estates are vast and include property north of the border."

"You would relinquish Stanton?"

"I may have no choice, as well you know."

Stanton understood the stakes, of course. And still he would join them. Lance almost could not believe what he was hearing.

"If not now, then never," Stanton said, his voice unwavering. Obviously the earl had given this much thought. He'd likely already considered rebellion long before Lance had approached him.

"Come back tomorrow at the same time. We will talk then."

Dismissed, Lance stood.

"You will find Stanton a new smith as well."

He nodded, not trusting his voice.

"Good day."

"Good day, my lord."

Lance left the earl, aware this was likely his last night at Stanton. He would speak to the boys and then . . . nay, Idalia would never see him.

But could he really leave without saying goodbye?

You are just like him.

Lance respected the earl, but he did not respect the way he treated his daughter. Attempting to talk to Idalia again would be a fool's errand. He had the earl's support and could not risk losing it.

Not even for her love.

❧ 24 ❧

"**Y**ou missed Guy by less than a fortnight."

Terric stretched his legs out in front of him, crossing his feet and arms simultaneously. It was the Scot's signature position, one Lance had seen many times over the years.

It meant his friend was thinking.

Which was just as well as Lance had been doing little else since leaving Stanton. It had taken just three days for him to travel to Dromsley Castle. Now that Terric was chief, he spent more time in Scotland than he did here in his English holding.

At least, he had before.

Now, with their mission solidified, Terric's second, his younger brother, would remain at Bradon Moor.

He was one of only a few who knew of their plan.

"What does he hope to accomplish?"

Terric sat up straight. "To defeat your quivering bastard of a king and see Louis on the throne."

Lance rolled his eyes.

"He is your king too. And no one is proposing to put the French king's son on the throne of England."

"I am."

Lance ignored that. "You've no need to make your

166

hatred of John known to me. But we did not form the order to overthrow the king."

Terric waved a dismissive hand. "But to temper his failed leadership and despotic rule. Aye."

Lance waited for Terric's mood to level out. He'd not lied to Stanton about Conrad's temperament. He was as measured as his father had been quick to anger. But Terric had a hot temper, easily sparked, and nothing made him angrier than the King of England and his men.

"You never told me of the earl's daughter," Terric said suddenly.

Lance ground his teeth, cursing Guy silently under his breath. He'd hoped his friend would keep that information to himself, although he wasn't exactly surprised to learn it wasn't so.

"There's nothing to tell."

"According to Guy, there's much to tell. He said you were in love with the lass."

"Guy is an arse."

"He would likely agree," Terric said, raising his brow. "But that doesn't make his claim false."

"We should discuss our plans. With Stanton's support—"

"*Lance.*"

There were times he was grateful for these men he called brothers, but other times he longed for the solitude that came with being a smith.

A position he no longer enjoyed now that he'd left both Bohun and Stanton. It had been agreed, months ago, that he would return here once he'd secured Stanton's support. He knew not what came next, but worrying about the future was futile since they may or may not still have their heads when this was over.

"Terric."

The chief frowned. "I am not Guy. You can speak to me of this."

The Scot did not intend to disparage their friend. He understood Terric's meaning. While Guy would never find himself at the mercy of love, or so he thought, Terric had already done so once before. He understood as well as anyone the pain of its loss.

"As I said—"

"You said there's nothing to tell. You're off your head if you think I believe that."

For such a large man, Terric could be surprisingly . . . gentle. But Lance really did not want to discuss Idalia.

Despite knowing his efforts would be futile, he'd tried to see her before he had left. Unsurprisingly, she'd refused him. Though he'd gained Stanton's support for their cause, he had lost something even more valuable.

"She is . . . remarkable," he found himself saying. "When I arrived, her mother was very ill. Thankfully, a physician arrived from London just before I left. It seems the skullcap she'd been taking for her headaches was the cause of her condition. But in her absence, Idalia took her mother's place, since her older sister had married not long before," he explained.

"But you don't wish to speak of her. Lady Idalia?"

"Nay."

Terric cleared his throat.

"What is there to say? We spent some time together and . . ."

It was excruciating to talk about her, even in such general terms. Although he'd opened himself to Idalia, Lance was not a man accustomed to speaking about his feelings. Before meeting her, the only person he'd professed to love was his mother.

"We fell in love," he said, forcing the words out. Surely Terric would know better than to press.

"Hmmm."

Lance concentrated on the tapestry behind his friend's head. The lord's chamber was overly large but nearly always cold. Multiple tapestries attempted, futilely, to keep out the chill.

"If Guy sat here, having declared such a thing, I would tell him to continue as if he'd not met the lass. But you are not Guy."

"Thank the saints," he said, forcing a smile.

Terric did not return it. "I am sorry your station prevents you from being with a woman such as Lady Idalia," he said, his tone earnest.

Lance said nothing.

"'Tis unjust, but 'tis the way of things."

"Her mother gave her blessing," Lance blurted out.

As expected, that fact managed to surprise Terric.

"She learned of our . . . indiscretion and, for her own reasons, was not against the match."

"How odd."

"But the earl . . ." His voice trailed off.

Terric nodded, his expression understanding. "'Tis surprising he did not toss you from Stanton when he learned of it."

"He didn't."

"Pardon?" His friend leaned forward as if perhaps he'd misheard.

"He did not learn of it. I could not chance telling him. And, to my knowledge, neither Idalia nor her mother did either."

Lance attempted to appear casual, but the Scot's expression made his chest ache. The longing he'd suppressed these last days rushed over him in a suffocating wave.

"You must tell him," Terric said.

"No."

"Lance—"

"I will not risk this mission. For anything."

It was only this thought that had allowed him to do what was needed and leave her.

Terric ran both hands through his hair. "Guy said he'd never seen you so . . . at ease before as you were at Stanton."

Lance stood. "So?"

"You do not deny it?"

"Deny that Idalia made me feel whole? Nay, I will not. But we've more important matters to discuss."

"More important? Do you truly believe a man who risks losing his title and property, possibly his life, will change allegiances because a blacksmith dares to confess loving his daughter?" Terric stood with him, his voice rising. "You're an intelligent man. I know it well. Think about it for a moment."

All of the anger and frustration and thwarted love bubbled inside him, forming a toxic brew. "Think about it?" he shouted, something he rarely did. "I've done nothing else since meeting her. But I will not endanger our mission. And I'm surprised you'd have me do so."

He turned to leave.

"It's not our mission you endanger," Terric said.

The softness of his tone was more jarring than if he'd shouted back at him.

A chill ran through Lance's shoulders and into his arms. He sucked in his breath and let it out, not trusting himself to respond.

So he left.

Something he was quite good at doing. Except this time, he had a real life, one that he loved. One that was gone, for good.

❧ 25 ❧

I dalia wandered through the crowded stands in search of her sister. After asking a few merchants if they'd seen Lady Tilly, she finally decided to let her sister find her instead.

"Is this where you propose to place the covered stands?"

The voice, a sweet sound to her ears, came from behind.

"Aye, Mother." She spun around. "Do you think the idea has merit?"

"Very much so."

The lady of Stanton paused to run her hand along a slip of silk. The merchant came over at once, eyes full of eagerness, and they launched into conversation about his wares. The fabrics in his stall were beautiful, but it was a nearby table that caught Idalia's eye.

"These are lovely," she said to the man who stood behind it. The man Idalia had been determined to avoid all week.

Stanton's new smith.

Idalia was not sure how Lance had done it, but apparently he'd promised her father he would find them a new smith. And he had.

She'd welcomed the man to the castle, of course,

but had not once visited the forge. And although she had sought solace at the Small Tower for years, she found she could no longer go there. Even looking down toward Eller's Green assaulted her with unwanted memories. When the need to be alone overcame her, Idalia instead climbed the ramparts to the west, enduring the guardsman's uneasy glances. There was no tower to hide behind, but at least the wall-walk afforded her new views.

Ones that did not remind her of Lance.

"Many thanks, my lady," said the new smith.

The man was only a slight bit older than her father, but his hair was completely white. When he'd asked her mother for permission to sell some of his wares at the market, she'd granted it gladly.

Though he was a blacksmith, the man had knowledge of whitesmithing. The jewelry that sat before her was quite beautiful, in fact.

"I apologize for not coming to you sooner." She had no real reason to give him.

"No apologies are necessary, my lady."

Though Idalia involved herself less in the daily affairs of Stanton than she had when her mother was ill, it was true that Idalia continued to take on far too much. According to Tilly, at least. Just that morning her sister had begged her to allow Mother to purchase for Stanton. "Go to market day unfettered, just for you," she had said.

If only she could be as carefree as that.

"If I could commission one of these"—she picked up a bracelet—"from you?"

"It would be my honor, my lady."

"The old smith was nearly as skilled," her mother said from behind her. "He made this, in fact."

Idalia did not realize her mother wore Lance's bracelet under her long sleeve. Taking it off, she showed the new smith.

"Fine handiwork indeed," he said, handing it back to her. "But that is to be expected. Master Lance apprenticed for one of the greatest smiths of our time."

"You knew his father?" Idalia asked before thinking better of it.

"Indeed. A great smith."

But not a good man, she added silently.

He attempted to hand the bracelet back to her mother, but she'd already hurried off to greet an old friend. Putting it on her wrist, she allowed herself to wander through the stands, although she acquired some much-needed spices for the kitchens instead of browsing for her own enjoyment.

Later, when it was time to leave, she finally found her sister.

"Where have you been?"

Tilly shoved a handful of ribbons at her. The silk strands of color caressed her hands as she stared at them.

"Look at this shade of blue. Have you ever seen anything so lovely?"

Shaking her head, Idalia walked toward the stables.

"I have not. Have you seen Mother?"

"Idalia, *look*."

There was nothing there but ribbons. She glanced at her sister in confusion.

"At?"

"You answered before you even looked at it. Will you be like this much longer? 'Tis frustrating."

"Be like what, my dear?" their mother said, joining them.

"Moving through life as if she is not a part of it."

Idalia rolled her eyes.

"You will give Mother a headache with your riddles," she scolded.

Thankfully, her mother had experienced no further head pain since she'd stopped taking the skull-cap. Just as the physician had predicted, Mother's ailments had abated within days. Though she still appeared frail, her coloring had improved. And most importantly, she felt wonderful. As if she'd woken from a horrible nightmare.

Ironically, though her father had refused to do so before, Father Sica's apparent disbelief that her mother was healed without his intervention was his undoing. He sent the priest away with enough coin to placate him after the harsh words Idalia had long hoped would precede his departure.

"'Tis not so much a riddle but a fact. Since Lance left, you have not been yourself."

Tilly, it seemed, knew more than expected. Idalia avoided her mother's eyes. Her mother had tried to speak with her about Lance, but she refused to discuss what had happened with him.

She was embarrassed. Hurt. Angry. But most of all, so very, very sad.

"I asked you not to speak of him."

"And I would gladly listen if I had my sister back."

"Perhaps she would come back if someone would stop reminding her of a certain smith."

"Come." Mother took each of them by the hand. "We will go back to the keep and sit in the garden. The weather is too beautiful for such arguments."

Indeed, the sun was showing itself for the first time in three days.

"There'll be no more talk of headaches," Mother continued, looking at her, "or men."

Which suited her well. If she never again heard the name Lance in her lifetime, it would be too soon. He was gone, never to return.

Unfortunately, he'd taken her heart with him.

❧ 26 ❧

"Idalia." Her father stopped her as she made her way from the hall. "I would speak to you in the solar."

She looked back to where her mother and sister were seated. Still at the head table. Still finishing their meal. She hadn't even noticed her father behind her.

"But your meal . . ."

"I would speak to you now," he repeated.

What could she do but follow him?

He led the way to his solar, and she fell in beside him, deep in thought about her problem.

Though she was beyond grateful for her mother's improvement—and for her father's reengagement in life at Stanton—she found it difficult to carry on as if all were well.

I wish I'd never met him.

It wasn't the first time she'd had that uncharitable thought, but she didn't quite believe it. Despite everything that had happened, despite the hurt that made it difficult to get out of bed in the morning, Idalia was grateful to have fallen in love with the blacksmith. To have known his touch, his love. He had made her feel as if she were someone special, and listening to him, she could almost believe she was as worthy of nurturing as Stanton's people.

Tilly had been telling her as much for some time.

They reached the solar, and her father waved her inside. "Sit," he commanded. She did, sighing inside. Idalia was certain her father didn't realize how harsh he sounded at times. "It is his way," her mother had always told her.

"I had hoped you would recover before now," her father said once they were both seated, he behind his desk, she in front of it.

"Recover?"

"From the smith."

He said it without mirth, straight-faced and serious.

"Father, I . . ." She stopped. What could she possibly say to that?

Had her mother told him? She'd assured Idalia she would not. So how did he know?

She crossed her hands on top of each other.

"I do not understand," she said, forcing an even tone. "The blacksmith is long gone from Stanton, and he found a suitable replacement, just as you requested. In fact, just the other day at the market I spoke with the new smith. His work is nicely done—"

"You had affection for him, did you not?"

"He is much too old," she said, deliberately misunderstanding.

Idalia had managed to force a rare smile from her father's lips. "Wayland. Not the new smith."

"How . . ." Nay, that would be admitting the truth. "I'm unsure how to respond, Father."

She uncrossed her hands, laying them on her lap, and stared down at them, hoping for some divine intervention.

"You've resisted every match thus far."

"You have been lenient with me, Father."

It was true. He had not forced her to marry against her will. Not yet, anyway. And Roysa had, in the end, married a man she loved, or thought she loved, if Mother was to be trusted. That they had any say in the matter was unusual. She suspected it was her mother's doing, especially after hearing about the man she had loved and lost.

"I have." He cleared his throat and looked over her shoulder. Idalia spun in her seat, but there was nothing there.

He seemed uncomfortable and out of sorts. Unusual for a man who was typically very self-assured.

"Is all well, Father?"

"We shall see. The smith," he continued. "Would you have taken him for a husband?"

Again, she stumbled on her words. "I . . . but . . ." Idalia took a deep breath. Somehow, he knew, and she could not deny it, not when the truth thrummed inside her, aching to be released. "Aye, I would have taken him for a husband."

"Despite the lies he told?"

So Mother *had* told him. It was quite unlike her mother to break a confidence in such a manner, but there was no other explanation.

"I would have taken him as a husband"—she frowned—"before I learned he was here only for your support."

"You do not approve of our alliance?"

A rather strange question from a man who rarely asked for her opinion and had never seemed to care about securing her approval.

"I do. And can understand his methods," she admitted.

"Then?"

"He claimed to love me, and yet he waited until the last possible moment to share his true purpose with me," she blurted out, her cheeks flaming with heat. If she thought it difficult to speak of such things with her mother, this was much, much worse.

"These are serious actions with even more serious consequences. For the blacksmith and for us."

As if she did not understand her father, and Stanton by extension, flirted with treason.

"Aye, Father."

Her hand found its way under the long sleeve of her gown to the bracelet she'd been loath to take off since her mother had abandoned it at the market. She knew her mother had likely not forgotten it—that she'd given it to her as a remembrance—yet she had not found the strength to give it back.

Twisting it, she waited, trying to understand what her father wanted from her or hoped to gain from this discussion. So he knew of Lance. And yet he'd not condemned her as a fool.

He'd not reacted as she'd feared.

"I would see you betrothed," he said finally.

Her head shot up. "Nay!"

"It is time for you to marry," he continued as if he'd not heard her. "Tilly will soon be of age."

"Nay," she repeated. "She is still a child."

But it was untrue. She'd seen the signs, even if she wished to ignore them. And she'd always known this day would come. When her father stopped asking and began demanding.

"There is one man who asked for my permission, and despite the circumstances, I plan to give it."

Twisting the bracelet faster and faster, Idalia desperately tried to think of an argument. Did her mother know of his plan? Why had she not warned her?

"Please, Father."

Not yet. Not when her heart was still broken.

"You do not even ask his name."

She didn't care who he was. Idalia would not

marry a stranger, no matter how handsome or powerful or kind.

"Please . . ."

"I may reconsider if you answer me honestly. I've just one question remaining."

Idalia nearly fell off her chair. He would reconsider?

Her mother's illness and recovery truly had changed the man she'd thought she knew.

"Do you love the smith?"

"Lance?"

She realized her mistake immediately. "That is to say, Master Lance?"

Her father just looked at her pointedly, waiting for an answer.

She could not look her father in the face and lie to him. Nor did she wish to lie to herself. So, after a moment's hesitation, she nodded. "Aye, Father. I love him still."

And hated herself for doing so.

"But what does this have to do with my betrothal?"

He lifted his chin, as if telling her to look behind her. Idalia knew what she'd see before she turned around. In truth, she should have known earlier, only she'd long since stopped hoping she'd see him again.

Hope could be a double-edged sword, after all, when the thing one hoped for never came to pass. And yet, she turned in her chair, and there he was—his frame filling the doorway as it had done at the forge.

"How long have you been standing there?" she managed.

"Long enough."

She was taking in his appearance, his freshly washed hair that was still damp. The surcoat that made him look more like a knight than a blacksmith.

And then her father's meaning finally registered. She whipped back around to face him.

"The man you would have me betrothed to?"

"Stands behind you even now."

He was serious.

Suddenly, Idalia realized her mother had not betrayed her confidence after all. Lance himself had told her father everything.

"He has asked to marry me?" she clarified, as if Lance were not in the room.

"He has."

Her eyes widened. "And you have given your permission."

"Aye."

She had so many questions. But *Why?* did not seem appropriate, nor did blurting out, *But he is a blacksmith.*

Unless . . .

"Did you consult with Mother about his request?"

Her father stood, giving her that strange and disarming half smile again. "I did," he admitted. "I will leave you to a discussion."

Idalia stood when he did.

"Mind you, you're only to have a discussion," he told Lance as he left. "Do you understand?"

Lance bowed his head as the earl passed him. "Indeed, my lord."

"Before you give your answer, daughter, you may want to look at that bracelet you're wearing a bit closer." With that strange remark, he stepped out of the room, giving Lance a final "Good eve, sir," before he closed the door behind him.

Sir.

He had been Sir Lance Wayland all along. So many lies.

So very much to discuss.

And then she reached for the bracelet.

❧ 27 ❧

"**G**ood den, my lady."

"I'm not sure that it is, *Sir* Lance."

She could breathe. In and out. It should be a simple matter.

"I'm hoping to change your mind about that," he said, his eyes peering into hers.

When he took a step toward her, Idalia stood firm. He'd hurt her, horribly. And a few honeyed words would not make things right.

"You are angry, rightly so. But know this. If it takes an evening, a fortnight, a sennight, or a year . . . it matters not. I aim to make you my wife. You told your father you loved me still, which gives me the hope I need, though don't deserve."

So he had heard her.

Those were some sweet words, indeed. But even so . . .

"I told him that," she began, still grappling with everything that had changed in the last minutes. "Because it is true. But marry you? Lance, you lied to me from the moment we met."

His jaw flexed, and Idalia hated herself for the thoughts that ran through her head. The source of her anguish stood before her, but all she could think of was touching him and being touched by him.

"No less than I lied to myself. I never thought to marry, but meeting you, loving you . . . Idalia"—he took another step toward her and stopped—"you give of everyone and ask for nothing for yourself. Let me be the one to give you something back. Let me love you as I should have done from the start."

She reached into her sleeve, twisting the bracelet around and around.

"How can I trust you?"

Lance shook his head. "It is not for you to trust me but for me to earn back that trust. I'm sorry that I tossed it aside so carelessly."

"A part of me," she admitted, "can understand why you did so. But if you'd just told me . . ." She shook her head. "A knightly order. A rebellion against the king. 'Tis nothing I've not heard before."

His eyes widened.

"I'm jesting." She smiled. "Your mission is an honorable one, though no less dangerous for its ambitions."

Lance smiled back, which was the precise moment Idalia knew she was lying to herself. He would win her over. He'd already done so.

"I offer little, as your father knows already. A blacksmith by trade, an absent husband—"

"Absent?"

"Our mission is far from over. With your father's support, we have some of the coin we need, and a few of the other Northern lords have already pledged their support, but to bring a king to heel is no small feat."

"And you would propose to do this . . . without me?"

"I'd never put you in danger by taking you with me."

She looked away from him, her shoulders sinking in defeat. It was just as she'd thought—even now, after everything, he would not confide in her.

Idalia only looked up when Lance stood immediately before her. Close enough to touch.

"You said I was just like him"—he lifted her chin—"but I am not. If you would come with me, then I would gladly have you by my side. As long as you understand the danger. But it is your choice. It will always be your choice, Idalia, because your thoughts have as much weight as my own."

"You would take me with you?"

"Of course."

"And seek my counsel?"

"Always."

She looked into his eyes. Before she knew it, Lance had reached under her sleeve and grabbed her wrist. That simple touch was enough to set her heart racing, and she startled when he pulled back her sleeve.

"Your mother gave it to you?"

He unclasped the bracelet and took it from her.

"For a time, aye."

He lifted it so she could see more closely.

"Good, for it is yours."

Her eyes narrowed. "What do you mean?"

"Did you see this?"

Idalia looked at the engraving that she and her mother had noticed that first day.

"Aye. We wondered about that from the start."

"Look closer. What do you see?"

She did as he asked. "'Tis a circle."

"Closer."

It was difficult to concentrate standing so near him. Idalia breathed in all that was Lance and attempted to see something more. For the first time, she noticed the faintest of lines around the circle.

"Lines. Faint ones. 'Tis the sun," she realized.

Lance took her hand, but true to his word to her father, he did nothing more than place the bracelet back around her wrist, his touch gentle.

"'Tis the sun," he confirmed.

And she understood.

The bracelet had not been for her mother after all.

Idalia. The meaning of her name was "behold the sun."

"You made this for me."

He nodded.

"I did."

Idalia grabbed his hand before he could pull it away.

⚜

LANCE TOUCHED HIS FINGER TO HIS LIPS. SHE'D kissed his fingers briefly. Moments later, a knock had landed on the door, after which it had burst open to admit Tilly, who had apparently learned of his visit from their mother. When Lady Stanton had arrived to retrieve her, his reunion with Idalia had turned into a family gathering. And though she'd softened a bit when he told her of the bracelet, she was still angry with him.

Which was why he was roaming the halls of Stanton in the dead of night. He knew he should return to the bedchamber the seneschal had installed him in after he first spoke to Lord and Lady Stanton. If the earl caught him out here at this time of night, there would be no way to explain his presence in the corridors.

Except he still needed to speak to Idalia.

She had not accepted his offer of marriage.

They'd agreed to talk on the morrow, and yet, he found he could not wait.

Lance cursed his decision not to take a torch or candle with him. Having worked in darkness his entire life, Lance could easily navigate it when he knew his surroundings. Stanton Castle was not so familiar. Still, Idalia's maid had given him directions to her chamber door, and it was blessedly in a separate tower from her parents.

He'd come to Stanton with every expectation that he'd be turned away. Still, Terric's words had refused to leave him. If he didn't try, he'd regret it always. And so he'd come. He'd been pleasantly surprised when he was granted an audience with both lord and lady. Lady Stanton appeared the very picture of health compared with the woman whose sickbed he'd visited.

He'd delivered his case to the couple, Lady Stanton had whispered something in her husband's ear, and a moment later, the earl had nodded at him. "A man who risks his life for justice, be he a great lord or tradesman, is worthy of my daughter."

Another whispered word from wife to husband.

"You will, of course, need her permission."

"Of course," he'd said, thanking the earl. And his wife, the person truly responsible for such a miraculous decision.

He'd left the meeting full of hope for the future, but later that eve, when he'd stood outside the earl's door, waiting for Idalia to possibly denounce him, he'd realized his work was not done.

He would secure her good opinion again if it was the last thing he did.

Cursing again as he reached her chamber door— at least he hoped it was her chamber door, although Leana's instructions had been quite thorough—he knocked softly.

Idalia opened her door almost immediately, indicating sleep had not come quickly for her either. His eyes inadvertently slipped down to her nightclothes, a simple cream chemise.

"I've never seen your hair braided before."

"You've never visited my bedchamber before."

Certainly not.

"May I come in?"

If he was caught here in the hall, it would not endear him to the earl.

When she opened it wide for him to enter, Lance did not take the gesture for granted. He intended to tell her everything he'd kept from her, including every single feeling he'd held back.

"Idalia, I've so much to tell you," he said as he stepped inside.

She closed the door behind him.

"I would prefer you did not."

His chest constricted.

"You hate me. Understandably."

"Hate you? Nay, I could never hate you." Her laughter, so genuine and spontaneous, surprised him. "But you misunderstand me. I'd rather you not tell me how you feel . . ."

She bit the side of her lip, a gesture that shot straight down to his cock, but Lance didn't allow himself to interpret the gesture—and the leading remark—as he'd like.

"I'd prefer it if you showed me."

He sucked in a breath. "Idalia," he ground out. "I did not come here with the intent to seduce you."

True enough, but she was making it difficult not to do so. When she looked at him that way . . .

"Pity."

Idalia turned and walked toward the hearth, stooping to put another piece of wood in the flames.

He stood at the door, mouth open, more surprised than when her father had agreed to allow him to court her.

Who was this woman?

Certainly not the one who had so tentatively touched her lips to his that first time.

And yet . . . Lance had known from the start there was a passion in her. Idalia just needed someone to trust. To allow her to relax, taking care of her as she did everyone else.

He was that someone.

He may not have come to seduce her, but by God that was exactly what he would do.

❧ 28 ❧

Was she still angry?

Aye, but Lance would not be leaving Stanton Castle again without her.

Idalia sensed him standing behind her, but it wasn't until she felt the braid being lifted off her back that she realized how close. A moment later, her hair fell against her back, the blue ribbon that had tied it together slipping onto the ground.

Pushing aside the very tresses he'd just released, Lance leaned closer. So close, she could feel his breath on her neck from behind.

"Show you?" he whispered. "Aye, I would gladly show you." The kindling she'd added to the fire released a loud, resonant crackle as his lips finally touched her neck.

"I would gladly show you," he whispered as he continued to trail featherlight kisses down her neck, her ear, "how sorry I am for not telling you sooner."

His mouth lowered to the soft spot just behind her ear as his hands reached around to cup her breasts. Needing to see him, Idalia turned in his embrace. He kissed her so passionately, she could not catch her breath. Nor did she wish to. She poured all her emotion into that kiss—every tear she'd cried, every morning she'd awoken bereft from longing—and knew he was doing the same.

They came together desperately, but soon their kiss was much more. With just the thin chemise between them, Idalia could feel everything.

Lance reached down to the hem of her chemise, lifting it off in one swift motion. She wore nothing under it, and for a moment, he stepped back and stared at her. There was ample light in the chamber from the fire and wall torches for her to see the awe and reverence in his face.

"You look at me as if you've never seen a woman as such before."

His eyes narrowed.

"Nay, I don't want to know."

"No woman matters but you."

Lance tore off his shirt, revealing those arms she'd admired so many times before in the forge.

Reaching out, she indulged herself, sliding her hand from the marking on his bicep upward.

"I'm glad you left your surcoat behind."

When he pulled her close once again, their bare skin touched, his chest hard against hers. And then he was kissing her again, his hands roaming from her back to her backside.

And that's when she realized it.

This man, this big, handsome man would be her husband. He would be hers, and she would be his. Tonight and forever after.

"Your skin is so . . . ," she murmured when his lips left her to explore, "warm."

He smiled down at her and then swooped her up off her feet—"Oh!"—carrying her like a babe to the bed. His immense strength was belied by the gentleness with which he laid her down. The tenderness with which he regarded her.

Undressing himself, Lance never took his eyes from hers.

When his manhood sprang free, her eyes widened.

Idalia knew how this was supposed to work, but suddenly she could not imagine it.

She didn't say so, but somehow he understood.

"Don't worry," he said, kneeling between her legs. Both hands rested on her breasts. "When it's time, you'll understand how 'tis possible."

Lance began to move both thumbs, rubbing small circles at first. And then he pinched her, hard enough that Idalia arched her back.

"In fact, you will want nothing more"—his fingers traced a path around the top of each breast and down to her waist—"than to feel me inside you."

His talented fingers lingered on her hips, though she willed them to pleasure her as they'd done before.

"Nay, my sweet sun." He reached under her knees. "My hands will stay right here, content to let my mouth play its part."

She understood his words just as Lance lowered his head between her legs.

So he'd not spoken false. This was truly happening.

The feeling was so unusual that she tried to close her legs.

"Nay," he said, opening them again, his warm breath tickling her.

Once again, Lance lowered his head. His tongue and mouth were even more talented than his fingers, it turned out, and this time, she nearly screamed in encouragement.

"If you ever stop," she said as he continued, "I will tell the king himself of your plans."

He swirled and teased, and Idalia could not seem to stop talking.

"Of course, I'd never do such a—oh my!"

Idalia let go of the poor, abused coverlet and attempted to hold on to Lance instead. Her fingers gripped both of his shoulders, and when he moaned, she arced up off the bed.

"That feeling," she said, gripping more tightly. "'Tis there, so close."

Despite her threat, he stopped.

Before she even had an opportunity to chastise him, Lance had shifted his position. He now lay on top of her, his body propped on his elbows.

"That feeling . . ." He stared at her so intently, she almost forgot to look down.

Almost.

"That feeling is a release of pleasure. As your husband . . ." He smiled. A beautiful, rare, smile. "I vow it will happen often."

When he guided himself toward her, Idalia gripped his wrists. She knew what would come next, courtesy of Roysa, but hearing of it was very different than the actual act.

"Think of how you felt a moment ago, with my lips on you."

Idalia looked at those lips now. The very recent memory came back quickly.

"It will hurt for a moment." He entered her then, and she forgot about his lips. Looking down at where they were joined, her eyes widened.

It didn't hurt at all. It felt odd. Intimate. But there was no pain.

"Look at me."

She did.

"I love you, Idalia."

With that, he kissed her. Hard.

The sensation of him inside her, his bare chest against her, his kiss . . .

And then he thrust in more deeply and Idalia broke off the kiss.

"That *did* hurt!"

His eyes were full of concern. "I'm sorry," he said, rubbing the back of his hand against her cheek. "I am sorry. But it will not pain you for long."

Indeed, it did not.

She clenched against him and nearly laughed at the expression on his face. Lance looked as if he were in pain. But she was no fool. Idalia knew he restrained himself—something he need not do any longer.

"The pain. 'Tis subsiding."

She smiled at his obvious relief.

"'Tis pleasant enough," she said.

Although it wasn't exactly what she'd expected, she savored the closeness to him.

His knowing look put a bigger smile on her face. "There's more?" she guessed.

Lance began to move. "Aye. There's more."

Slowly at first, the muscles in his arms straining as he kept himself lifted above her, Lance pulled himself out.

And then he pushed back in a bit more quickly, his grin unlike any she'd seen before.

"Oh!" she gasped. "That's more than pleasant."

In response, Lance reached between them, somehow holding himself up with one arm, and Idalia was lost.

She met his movements, pressing herself into his fingers. Into *him*.

With each thrust, she felt his desperation. His love. She'd lost more than her maidenhood this night.

She'd lost the self-doubt that had made her feel she didn't deserve to be cherished in the way she cherished other people.

"We will never be apart again," she said, Lance never taking his eyes from her.

"Never," he agreed.

"I am so close to . . . something."

"Coming. You can say it."

He circled his hips, his thumb pressing against her.

"You can say anything to me, Idalia."

He thrust hard then, and she was lost. When he moved his hand back to the bed, Idalia reveled in the sensation of being trapped between his two massive arms.

Every muscle clenched together. Her legs, her buttocks. So tight, even her eyes squeezed shut. She made a sound that was hard to believe came from her lips.

And there it was.

Idalia opened her eyes, wanting to see him, and stared at his face. Mouth open, head back, he found his pleasure too.

In her.

It was the most glorious, most powerful feeling in the world. She would hold him to his promise to ensure it happened often.

Collapsing on her, Lance kissed her lips and then her neck.

She wrapped her arms around him, or tried to at least, as the final pulses of pleasure ebbed away.

"I never want to move," she said.

In response, he did move, just slightly. Idalia sighed.

"More than pleasant?" He lifted his head.

"Much more."

She looked into his eyes then, knowing there was still much that troubled him. But at this moment, her blacksmith was content.

"I love you," she said, aware she'd not said the words aloud before.

She was about to say more when an insistent knock on the door startled them both.

"I'm glad to hear it," Lance said, pulling away, "before I die."

Idalia wanted to reassure him otherwise, but as she scrambled to dress, she feared his assessment might be quite accurate.

❧ 29 ❧

He'd had a good life. Finding Idalia, falling in love . . . it was more than he'd ever hoped for. As he reached for the iron handle of Lord Stanton's solar, a fine piece of craftsmanship, Lance resigned himself to the fact that this may very well be it for him.

Not that he blamed the earl.

If he had a daughter and a man who was not her husband snuck into her bedchamber and took her virginity, he'd likely kill the fool too.

The poor maid. Leana had been mortified to fetch him in Idalia's bedchamber, knowing where he would be found.

The earl had bade her fetch him, saying he wished to speak to him immediately.

"Good eve, my lord," he said, admiring how well lit the chamber was compared to the dark corridors. There were at least ten wall torches bracketed around the ceiling of the circular room.

"I am in here often," he said by way of explanation for the lighting. He gestured for Lance to take a seat. "Even at night."

"You wished to see me?"

He didn't look like a man who was about to end

his life, but Lance knew better than to trust appearances.

"I apologize for the hour. But we have much to discuss."

"Indeed."

So he had not brought him here to kill him? Or to toss him in Stanton's dungeons?

Perhaps he didn't know after all.

"You will be wed to my daughter, then?"

They'd not actually discussed the wedding, but after this night, it was a certain outcome.

"Aye, my lord."

"There is the matter of her dowry."

"I do not expect her to have one, my lord. I bring little enough to this union, as you are aware."

Stanton sat back in his chair, pointing to the pitcher in front of him.

"Wine?"

He nodded.

As Stanton handed him a goblet, he continued. "You offer her protection. And love." The earl shifted, clearly uncomfortable with that last sentiment. "But she has been raised with a certain level of ... comfort."

Stanton took a sip of his wine, so Lance did the same. "Her dowry will include Tuleen Castle."

"Just on the other side of Stanton's village?"

He'd seen it on the way here, a handsome structure.

"Aye. As well as the income from the market."

Lance nearly dropped his wine. That was no small gift, and both men knew it well.

"Idalia has some ideas for expansion. Of course, with events unfolding as they are ..."

The earl offered much more than he could have imagined, certainly more than he would ever need. He cared only for Idalia. And for keeping his head after this rebellion. Those were the only two things that mattered.

Lance should likely not say what he was thinking, especially in light of the earl's generosity. And yet, Idalia had made herself quite clear, and the earl would discover his daughter's intention soon enough anyway.

"She aims to come with me, my lord."

His words had precisely the effect Lance had expected. Thankfully, the seneschal chose that moment to open the door.

"Pardon, my lord. Would you care for more wine?"

Stanton did not answer. The seneschal took that as a sign to leave, but Lance stopped him.

"If I may ask a favor, sir?"

Dawson nodded.

"Will you send for the Lady Idalia please?"

Dawson glanced at the earl, who nodded tightly, and then back at him.

"Very good." With a small bow, he left.

And Lance was left alone, once again, with the Earl of Stanton.

And his anger.

"She will not."

Before he'd met Conrad and Terric, Lance would have been terrified to address an earl in so bold a manner. But his friends had taught him to see beyond titles and holdings. Conrad and Terric were lords, aye, but they were also simply men.

The same ones who jested and drank with him. Who talked of pretty women and practiced their swordplay with him and Guy.

Stanton was an earl, aye. But he was also a man.

"Your daughter is one of the most intelligent women I've ever met. Strong and independent, she is extraordinary, as you know."

"Which is why she will not be thrown into the middle of a rebellion against the king."

"I would have her stay at Stanton, or Tuleen, as well. But she has indicated her intention to do otherwise. And I must respect that."

Stanton slammed down his goblet.

"You must respect me. And I say she will not go with you."

Lance could not change this man's thinking any more than he could change his own father. They believed differently about Idalia's role, a woman's role—and the earl's beliefs were likely as deeply rooted as his own.

But he could try, at least, to make him understand his thinking.

"You said Idalia has ideas for the market. Are those more valid than the ideas she has on where to go? How to live?"

"You push your luck, smith."

He did indeed.

Then again, he'd been doing so from the first moment he stepped foot in Stanton Castle, and it hadn't failed him yet.

"I am the same man to whom you pledged your support. And your daughter's hand in marriage. Trust that your judgement is sound, and I will not disappoint you."

Lance silently thanked Guy for his lessons on logic and argument. Without them, he'd have already been tossed from the chamber.

As Stanton continued to glare at him, he took a sip of the fine red wine.

Lance was sure the earl would rebuke him again, but when the door slammed open behind him, both men turned to stare.

Idalia had arrived.

"Please do not be angry with him," she said to her father, his dark expression as fierce as she'd feared it would be. She'd been on her way down to the solar when Dawson caught up with her.

She was prepared to continue when Lance caught her eye. He shook his head ever so slightly. At first she thought he wanted to silence her—a thought that summoned a spurt of anger—but she quickly remembered Lance was not her father. He was attempting to tell her something.

She trusted him, so she stopped talking and waited for her father to respond.

"He tells me you plan to accompany him?"

Her father dared her to refute the words, but she would not.

Did he know Lance had been in her bedchamber?

"We've not discussed it in great detail just yet."

Or even a wedding. They'd been otherwise occupied.

"You will not go with him."

Her shoulders slumped at his tone. His words, as always, were final.

Idalia looked at Lance as she moved toward him. Forgetting to be embarrassed after what had passed between them, she thought instead of all he'd endured at the hands of his father. It was true hers could be difficult, but he had never once raised a hand against anyone in their family. Never would. But his treatment had hurt her in other ways, and the time had come to stand her ground.

Instead of bowing her head, as she'd normally do, she raised her chin. "I *will* go with him," she said, speaking as if she were the earl instead of merely his daughter. "You've given your blessing to him, a man you hardly know. Now give it to me, your daughter, whom you know is capable."

She spoke the truth and had proven as much during her mother's illness.

"Let her go."

They all turned at the sound of her mother's voice.

Entering the room, the countess strode up to her husband. She smiled at Idalia and Lance, offering her encouragement.

This was certainly not the first time the countess had disagreed with her husband, but it was only one of a few times she'd done it so openly. It was simply not her mother's way.

"She will be in danger," her father said, his voice betraying his typical stalwart manner.

"Nay," Lance interjected. "She will not. The Order of the Broken Blade will protect her."

Her father seemed to understand, but Idalia did not. Order of the Broken Blade? The rebellion? Likely, but what was the significance of such a name?

They stared at one another, her father seeming to take Lance's words into consideration. She could have left it at that, and perhaps he would have capitulated, but while she appreciated Lance's assistance and her mother's support, this was her argument to be won.

"I love you, Father," she said. Words she had spoken to him far more often than he did to her. "You have always protected us, and you've taught me the values of justice and nobility. I will carry those lessons with me as I do my part to protect Stanton and its people from the king."

Her mother winced.

"By Lance's side. I will marry him, and together, we will do what is necessary. But I am going with him."

"I promised Tuleen Castle as a part of your

dowry." Her father's eyes narrowed. "And I can take it away."

Tuleen Castle. She had always wondered about her dowry. The thought of living there with Lance, so close to her mother and Tilly . . .

But she would not be bought with the promise of anything.

"Do what you must."

Her mother sucked in a breath, but Idalia's gaze was fixed on her father.

Daring him to deny her.

She'd seen him negotiate many times, and one thing she'd learned was the importance of follow-through. If necessary, she would marry Lance without her father's blessing. Leave Stanton Castle with nothing.

"She will stay in the north," her father commanded.

"Aye, my lord," Lance agreed.

"If John retains these French mercenaries—"

"He will not."

"When the king learns of the rebellion, learns of its members . . ." Her father's voice trailed off.

Idalia shivered at the reminder of what they were talking about: rebellion against the king. And she would be in the middle of it, by choice.

"Clan Kennaugh will provide protection."

Clan Kennaugh. A border clan. Idalia had heard of them before but knew little else about them. She had so many questions, but only one that mattered now.

"Father," she cut in. "Will you trust that you have raised me well?"

He frowned, clearly displeased. But she already knew his answer.

❧ 30 ❧

I dalia dismounted, leading her horse into the deep thicket of trees. They'd agreed to leave the grounds of Stanton Castle before their discussion. One she'd been anticipating since their discussion in her father's solar last eve.

Her father had suggested they visit Tuleen Castle, with an escort of course. That escort, Tilly, had abandoned them as soon as they passed through the gatehouse. She'd remembered a "pressing matter" to which she needed to attend.

Idalia would have believed her if not for the wink Tilly gave her as she rode off. The gesture confirmed her assessment of her sister—Tilly was fast becoming a young woman. Idalia did not know what to make of it, but she supposed her opinion did not matter. Tilly would grow up whether she approved or not.

"Let me take him," Lance said, gathering the reins from her and leading her mount to the stream.

They had much to talk about.

She watched as Lance cared for the horses. For a man who spent his days hammering metal, he was surprisingly gentle. Her heart skipped a beat at the thought that they were finally alone together, completely and blessedly so.

After the tense talk with her parents last eve, her mother had whisked her away to her bedchamber. They'd spoken of posting banns and of the wedding, which they'd agreed should happen as quickly as possible.

Idalia and Lance would be leaving the moment the vows were exchanged, a fact that both scared and excited her. Despite her conviction to leave with Lance, she knew little of what she was running toward.

But that would change.

Now.

Lance tied off the horses and turned to her. If not for all of the uncertainty that still lingered between them, this could be the perfect day. It was certainly the perfect spot.

The sun actually shone through the clouds, and they were surrounded by willow trees. As soon as it had been decided they'd be visiting Tuleen this afternoon, she'd known exactly where she wished to stop. Although she'd expected a chaperone to be with them.

Thank goodness Tilly had decided to give them space.

Lance closed the distance between them in just a few strides. When he pulled her to him, his kiss was insistent and all-consuming. She returned it, for a time, but eventually pulled away.

"Sit with me," she said, gesturing to the bank of the river.

"With pleasure." Lance pulled out a small blanket from his horse's saddlebag. After spreading it out across the grass, he held out a hand to her.

"Do you always travel so prepared?" she asked as she sat with his assistance.

"Aye."

Idalia wasn't surprised by his answer. Lance did

always seem prepared for what lay ahead.

"What is the Order of the Broken Blade?" she blurted out.

Lance grabbed her hand and squeezed. She loved when he did that.

"Your father only knows that is an order of knights. Myself, Guy, Terric, and a man named Conrad Saint-Clair."

"The Earl of Licheford?"

"Aye, the same."

"And Terric?"

"Chief of Clan Kennaugh of Bradon Moor."

"The one you said would keep us safe, if need be?"

"Idalia." Lance squeezed her hand again. "I will keep you safe. You will not be in danger, ever. I promise you that. But if we need to take precautions, leave England for a time? Aye, Terric's clan will welcome us."

She still had so many questions.

"The four of us have pledged to end the king's reign. Or to at least force him to cease such policies as kidnapping for failure to pay exorbitant taxes."

"I mean no disrespect—"

"Why a blacksmith and a mercenary?"

She hadn't intended to ask that way, but it did seem a curious combination.

"We each have our reasons." Lance stood.

Idalia watched him take something from the same sack from which he'd removed the blanket. This was a hard object wrapped in a cloth. When he dropped it at her feet and then proceeded to sit beside her and unwrap it, Idalia did not know what to make of it. A sword hilt. Ornate, obviously of fine craftsmanship.

She looked up and waited for him to explain.

"I'd been attending the Tournament of the North with my father since I was able to ride. He serviced his lord, and others, as the tournament smith."

Idalia had heard of it, of course. Though she had never attended.

"I'd met Guy the year before. Each day, during the melee, my father gave me leave to walk the grounds as every knight would be on the field at that time. It was during one of these afternoons he and I wandered down to the riverbank."

Lance picked up the hilt.

"This was once Conrad's. Or his father's, to be precise."

Idalia did not interrupt even though dozens of questions flitted through her mind.

"We spotted two boys who appeared to be our age practicing with their swords. One, tall and thin. The other . . . just thin." He laughed. "When you meet Terric and Conrad, you'll never be able to imagine either of them as boys."

He smiled. Lance did not smile often, but whenever he did, it made Idalia's heart soar. Whoever these men were to him, he obviously cared very much for them.

"Even then, Guy was good with the sword. When he asked for a turn, the boys obliged easily despite the fact that we were obviously not noble like them."

"Licheford is the earl now, is he not?"

"Aye, a title he inherited from his father. Terric is also an earl."

Her brows drew together. The Scot was also an earl?

"Clan chief in Scotland, Earl of Dromsley in England."

Dromsley. She hated to interrupt again, but that name sounded familiar. She would ask about it later.

"But that summer they were both simply the sons of powerful men practicing with their swords."

As quickly as his smile had come, it went away. There was something darker to his story, as evidenced by the hilt he held in his hand and the troubled look on his face.

The loud call of a bird interrupted them. Watching as it flew by with its companion, Lance took up his story again.

"Guy heard the scream first. We could not see anything from where we stood, but the sound was easy enough to hear. By the time we reached the wooded area where it originated, Cait was lying on the ground, her gown lifted above her waist."

His hand gripped the hilt so tightly his knuckles had grown almost white.

"Terric roared, a sound that I will never forget."

He looked up, his eyes gleaming with unshed tears.

"A man, one of the king's men, held her down."

Idalia gasped. "He took her by force?"

"He was attempting to, aye. Thankfully, we arrived in time to prevent it."

She almost didn't want to know what had happened next. Looking at the hilt now, its lack of a blade began to make more sense.

Lance shook his head.

"It happened so fast. I ripped the man from Terric's sister . . ."

Idalia gasped.

"But he was much, much larger than any of us. One punch landed me on the ground. Terric lunged at him, getting between the man and his sister, but he was easily tossed aside as well. Guy was the first to draw blood, his quickness with a sword a boon for a short time until the guard grabbed his own weapon. From there, neither Guy nor Conrad stood a chance."

Obviously all four of them were alive now. Which meant . . .

"It was Conrad who killed him."

Lance lifted the broken hilt. "The guard broke

Conrad's sword with one strike. While he was engaged with Guy, Conrad slit the man's throat with the piece of blade that remained."

"But it is not there any longer? 'Tis only a hilt."

"Aye." He turned the hilt over in his hands. "When we tossed the guard's body in the river, this went with it."

The guard's body.

Idalia had suspected as much.

"It was only later, with clearer thinking, that I fetched it, realizing the discovery of Conrad's broken blade with the body would not bode well for him. I removed the remainder of the blade."

"And kept the hilt?"

He nodded. "Conrad wanted to be rid of it."

"So you took it? Kept it safe?"

Laying the hilt on the grass, he turned to her.

"Aye." Lance held her hand once more. "We vowed to keep that secret, and I've not told anyone since. Every year the four of us meet at the tournament. But we never discuss what happened with Cait and her attacker."

"Cait." She said the name, trying to imagine what the lady had endured, but it was too excruciating. "Is she well now?"

"Aye, according to Terric she is. I've not seen her since that day. Cait never returned to another tournament and remains in Bradon Moor. She refuses to even visit Dromsley Castle. She won't come back to England."

"I can understand her reason."

"It was a different king, of course—John's father—but it had an impact on all of us. Respect must be earned—it is not owed to a man simply because he's affiliated with the king."

"Your reason for the rebellion?"

"Nay. My reasons are simple. Conrad asked for our

support. And his cause is just. King John must be stopped."

Conrad willed it. It was the right thing to do.

Lance had no personal stake in this. He only did it to support his friend. His country.

He was exactly the man she'd thought him to be.

And he was hers.

"And now you have my support," she said. "Though it is a small victory, to be sure."

"A small victory? Idalia, how could you say such a thing?"

She'd just meant that she could do little in a rebellion against the king, but from his expression, Lance did not seem to agree.

The way he looked at her, with such love and longing, made her forget everything except for how blissful it had felt being joined with him the night before.

Lance must have been thinking the same. His eyes darkened. The air around them seemed charged with electricity. Their contemplation of the past had ended. They were right here, rooted in this very moment.

"Kiss me," she demanded.

He leaned forward.

"I'll gladly do that, and more, my sun."

"Soon to be your wife." Idalia smiled. "The wife of a blacksmith. I quite like it."

He was on top of her so quickly, Idalia didn't even have time to blink.

"I've many things to show you I think you'll like," he said, his voice low and incredibly seductive.

She did not doubt he meant every word.

"What, pray tell, are you waiting for?"

His laugh echoed all around them, the sweet sound a balm to her soul.

EPILOGUE

Idalia thought she felt air float over her body, where a moment ago she'd been warm, snuggled between her husband's body and the soft coverlet.

"What are you thinking of?" Lance asked.

Idalia opened her eyes.

She hadn't imagined it.

Her husband actually lay between her thighs, the coverlet pushed to the side. Blinking to clear away the remnants of deep slumber, she attempted to lift her head.

Lance pushed open her legs and kissed just above her knee. Another kiss, this one on her thigh.

"Terric."

He stopped his ministrations, and Idalia couldn't help but laugh at his expression.

"I wonder where he found this coverlet. 'Tis the softest I've ever felt. I may ask him if we can take it with us when we leave."

Of course, Lance had warned her that they might be at Dromsley Castle for some time. It was from here their order would conduct its missions. Owned by a Scot, the castle was apt to attract less attention than Conrad's home, Licheford, might.

"I'll need you to stop thinking of Terric," he said, resuming his ministrations.

"But he is quite nice," she said, attempting to bite back laughter.

"Nice," Lance grumbled. "Large. Terrifying. Those are the words more often used to describe the chief."

He was getting closer.

"Well, *I* believe him to be quite nice."

Lance had found his mark.

"Do you, then?"

He started with a quick kiss, but then his tongue darted out, finding exactly the right spot.

"And do you believe this to be quite nice?" he asked, repeating his actions.

Idalia lifted her hips toward his mouth, receiving a chuckle in response. She could no longer engage in conversation. Waking up this way . . . it would take some getting accustomed to, but Idalia was a quick learner.

As Lance became more insistent, Idalia attempted to keep her moans as quiet as possible. She did not know how easily sounds could be heard outside of their chamber.

"Oh!" But it was getting harder and harder to do.

Thankfully, Lance shifted his position, moving quickly up her body and covering her mouth with his own.

Kissing her, he guided himself inside.

The sensation of him inside her, filling her so perfectly, so completely, was such that Idalia knew she would not last long. She told him as much, and as always, it seemed to expedite his own pleasure. For just as she could feel the spasms overtake her, Lance cried out, though not so quietly as she.

Pulsating with him, her muscles went from tense to pudding. One moment she was tensing from head to toe, the next, Idalia could not have moved if the keep were attacked.

Gathering her in his arms, Lance pulled out and shifted them both to their sides.

"Good morn, wife."

She smiled. He'd said that every day since their wedding. She still loved the sound of the word on his lips.

"Good morn, husband. Or"—she loved to tease him—"my lord, if you prefer."

He rolled his eyes. "Husband, please."

"Why do you dislike the title?" she asked, her question an earnest one.

"'Tis not me. I am a smith. Will always be a smith."

He kissed her nose.

"A smith who is also a knight. And a lord."

"Husband is my greatest title."

And he meant it. Lance never let her forget how much he loved her. Even Terric had commented on his constant show of affection, saying, "Who is this man? Where is his scowl?"

Idalia closed her eyes, content to lie in Lance's arms just a bit longer.

Lance and Terric had both warned her the current calm would not last for long. In two days' time, they would ride out to speak to a border lord whose support was all but guaranteed.

And yet . . . one whispered word to the wrong person would see both men branded as traitors.

Idalia sighed heavily at the thought.

"Don't worry, my sun."

He could always tell what she was thinking. Idalia opened her eyes and met her husband's beseeching gaze.

"Once Guy sends those mercenaries back to France, which I'm sure he'll manage, John will be in a much weakened position. We nearly have the support we need to confront him. Before long, we'll be at Tuleen Castle, missing these adventures."

She traced his lower lip with her thumb. "Sending an army of mercenaries hired by the king back to France," she said. "Seems quite a mission for just one man."

He took her thumb in his mouth, as she'd hoped he would do.

"Thankfully, Guy is more of a man than any I know. He will not fail."

When he nipped her thumb and then licked the "wound," Idalia resigned herself to no more sleep that morn. If there was one thing she enjoyed more, however, it was this.

"I hope you are right," she said, putting Guy from her mind.

"I am." Lance captured her hand and pinned it behind her head. "Now, if you will, can we stop talking about the order? I prefer you to think of just one man when we are in bed."

"Oh? And which one would that be?"

He didn't answer. At least, not with words.

Idalia chuckled. "Thankfully, there is just one man for me."

JOIN OUR SECRET ORDER

We may not be knights intent on toppling a monarchy, but the Blood and Brawners are certainly one fun group of romance readers who enjoy being teased (actually, that drives them crazy but I do it anyway) and chatting all things romance and hunky heroes.

Facebook.com/Groups/BloodandBrawn

Not on Facebook? Get updates via email by becoming a CM Insider. Delivered bi-weekly, this includes "My Current Obsessions" as well as exclusive giveaways.

CeceliaMecca.com/Insider

ABOUT THE AUTHOR

Cecelia Mecca is the author of medieval romance, including the Border Series, and sometimes wishes she could be transported back in time to the days of knights and castles. Although the former English teacher's actual home is in Northeast Pennsylvania where she lives with her husband and two children, her online home can be found at CeceliaMecca.com. She would love to hear from you.

 facebook.com/ceceliamecca

 twitter.com/ceceliamecca

 instagram.com/ceceliamecca

Made in United States
Orlando, FL
20 September 2022